MONEYPENNY

THE MAGIC CAT

HELEN M. HOGAN

The Reading Glass Books
1-888-420-3050
www.readingglassbooks.com
production@readingglassbooks.com

DEDICATION/ ACKNOWLEDGEMENTS

Thanks to my Friends who helped me through the process:

Adebusola Halima Yusuff, my Alpha Reader, an extraordinary teenager living in Grand Prairie, Texas. She is smart enough to spot any confusing or boring passage, and politely bold enough to point it out.

Sherry Byars, assistant instructor with me in the Senior Department class at Tarrant County College, She offered not only moral support but performed miracles helping me retrieve documents.

Dani Howell, my horse friend for over forty years has become a computer expert who can teach me how to solve most of the weird puzzles my computer can throw at me.

Angela Bennet Redman, friend and photographer, who brings daughter Audrey for riding lessons and shares her skills with enthusiasm.

My dear husband, Berry Hogan, who reminded me when I worked too late. He couldn't get around as he once did, but patted my shoulder in encouragement. He is in a better place now.

Angel Yusuff, our home health lady who made life easier for both Berry and me. She watches out for him and she introduced Adebusola, her daughter to me.

TABLE OF CONTENTS

CHAPTER I
MONEYPENNY'S MISSING WINGS

She arrived breathless from the Rainbow Bridge, amazed the senior angel chose her.

She had not done anything heroic, nor learned great wisdom. Just a tiny tawny tabby girl, she'd lingered for her owner without much hope, for the lady had other cats and doubtless would own more in years to come. Hundreds of pets wandered over or around or even under the amazing glowing bridge. A few angels directed them without much explanation, "Wait here."

She hardly knew what she was waiting for, when a dark-haired angel in a worn white robe tapped her shoulder, saying, "You'll do. Climb the stairs or run up the bannister to the Golden Gates."

When she paused, he gently flicked her whip-like tail. "Go on, now. It's OK. He has a job for you."

"Who was 'He'? Surely not the One. I'm just a kitten, what could He want with me?"

"Good girl, MoneyPenny. We have work that requires your skill."

The little cat stared in amazement. A large angel in glowing robes leaned toward her with his hand out. Though he said no more, she knew he expected her to come to his fingertips. She glided quickly to his hand and lifted her face to touch her nose to his outstretched finger. She didn't know if it would be rude to mew to one so high in the ranks of Angelic hierarchy that she had never met one before.

"No, my dear little tabby, your thoughts are not rude. I am far from The One, though I feel His love. I'm sort of liaison agent with people who are so depressed that they are in danger of losing sight of that Love."

MoneyPenny feared she did not understand such an important job. Worst of all, she feared she could never do anything to help such important work.

"Come, Kitten, climb aboard," the angel said, opening his hand. It was large and smooth, but its palm wore callouses as if he had lifted heavy weights. The rough skin tickled her little paws as she walked into the center of his hand and felt warmth and safety she had never known before. She was lifting upward, but she knew no fear. The angel smiled at her as his old lips whispered a kiss to her softest fur, the golden light ring under her jaw and behind her ears. She felt her body vibrating, though barely. Was this a purr? She had not yet learned that skill.

The hand where she rested moved to snug against the sash around the High Angel's waist. The kitten's eye widened as she looked past the fold of robe to study the face. No beard, she noticed, and very dark complexion. Black kinky hair lay flat against his head, pulled back into what she heard some girls call a pony tail.

"Well, little Darlin', maybe I best explain a few things right quick. I was a black man when I was alive. The One is beginning a new program where our skin lightens gradually and their's tans. He doesn't want the sins of pride or racial prejudice to contaminate His angels.

Now one of my jobs for you to do, one that will take all of the first of your nine lives, is to save a lady from depression. She had a big Maine Coon cat named for a movie star from her youth—Tab Hunter. The cat did a foolish thing, darting out the door as someone came in.

He wanted to see and smell and taste the world outside the windows. Some neighbor dogs running as a pack, just working on their predatory instinct, killed him. She had raised him from a tiny kitten, told him all her problems, did her best thinking when she talked to him. Now she is sick with grief, hardly eating. Here is where you come in."

"But I'm not a healer, I haven't learned any magic yet."

"Ahh, Little MoneyPenny, don't get ahead of the story. We will put you in a place where she will see you. She will be attracted to your lovely tawny stripes. You will tell her that you can make her feel better."

"But I can't speak."

"He has blessed you with a special gift. You will be able to project your thoughts so that a person will clearly hear them." The dark-skinned one waved his other hand. "No such thing as language for thoughts."

MoneyPenny took a deep breath. How would she know what to say?

When the lady looks at you, and you will know her by her sad eyes, all you have to do is think, "If you take me home with you, I will make you feel better."

That didn't sound too hard, though she wondered how she could be sure she'd make her lady feel better. Then she felt the Angel's answer though she did not see his lips move: "As soft and pretty and tiny as you are, she will fall in love with you."

When she reached the landing at the top of the stairs and faced the huge and glowing Golden Gates, she gasped for breath. A new silvery angel stood by the gate. He bent down to meet her eyes. "I will take you to the shelter set up in the PetCo store. You will have a deluxe double condo in the adoption section."

By now she could not tell if he spoke to her or if she just "heard" him with her new power. Several events blurred in her perception. Then she woke up in a comfortable kitty bed with a bowl of kibbles beside it. Her bed faced some walls of lattice work. All very pretty, but she could not go anywhere. She tried to think if there was any place she needed to go. She did not remember any of the angels telling her she was going to some fancy kind of prison. Her room connected to three other rooms, one of them down a ramp and one she could access by climbing a cat tree pole. A lady put some fresh wet food into a bowl in her middle room.

"I'm told you are Penny. I'm here to help you find your perfect 'Forever Home.'"

MoneyPenny wondered. How long that would be, how she would recognize the person, and who this lady really was. The lady laughed. "You little Munchkin, I'm Ms. Alice, and I will help screen the people for you. I don't think you will be here long. You're too cute and smart."

At first she played, hopping or climbing from room to room, then took a nap sprawling across the luxurious cat bed with its red velvet cover. Soon she practiced her new thought reading skill. She also tried to answer the people's thoughts. Several customers murmured regrets that they could not take her home. Then She felt a general sadness and images of a very large, very fluffy tabby fellow flooded her mind. Then she saw the tabby coat ripped with his corpse under it.

MoneyPenny caught her breath, she had to hurry to attract the lady's attention. She scrabbled up the cat pole into the room that hung over the shopping aisle. She reached out with her right front paw toward the lady and concentrated:

"If you take me home with you, I will make you feel better."

The lady turned back. She read the letter Ms. Alice wrote for Penny. "You are lovely!"

She hurried away and returned with a clerk in PetCo uniform armed with a set of keys. They opened the kittycondo and reached in for her. Despite being unfamiliar with people up close, MoneyPenny walked into the lady's arms. The woman rubbed her face along the kitten's side and blew softly into the fur. MoneyPenny thought her happiest thoughts and relaxed into the lady's warm arms. She was pretty sure she saw one of her Angel sponsors looking in the window, sunlight shining through his body and wings.

When the lady came back with her husband and did some kind of paperwork with Ms. Alice, MoneyPenny thought her adventure was over. They put her in a carrier to take her home in the car. On the way, the strangest thing happened. The dark-skinned angel appeared in the back of the car, all crowded up. She heard his thought that she had work to do. In horror, she watched him shrink to a figure less than a foot tall and crawl into her carrier. His thoughts reassured her.

"But Ms. Alice is one of our ambassadors on earth, and she needs our help to find a home for two boy cats. You will have to help convince your new Mom to adopt them."

That seemed a huge problem because she didn't yet have any clout with her new Mom.

He explained the two are litter brothers and at 18 months have never been separated. The firstborn, a long-haired black cat, had a sinus infection Ms. Alice had been treating for a year.

MoneyPenny could not imagine even the nice lady adopting her would take in a cat already sick.

"You've got several months to figure this out, Little Darlin'. Maybe he will be well by then. Now, I've got to get out of here before I am stuck in this size." the dark angel thought to the little cat.

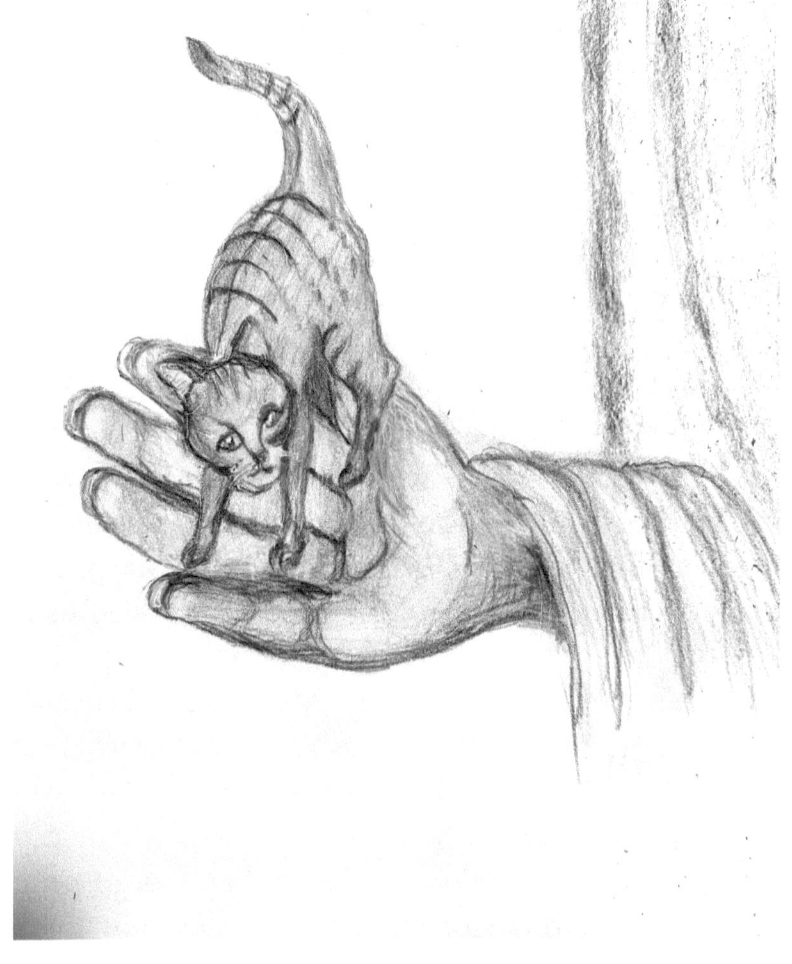

MoneyPenny giggled as his calluses tickled her pads.

CHAPTER 2

NEW FRIENDS

MoneyPenny and Ms. Marcy communicated mostly by thinking to each other. Ms. Marcy enjoyed telling the kitten how pretty she is and giving her treats and toys. MoneyPenny learned a new skill too. She found that she could hear both sides of telephone conversations just by rubbing her fur on Ms. Marcy as her lady held the phone. One of the people she talked to was Ms. Alice.

MoneyPenny liked the way Ms. Alice talked about the cats she fostered and the ones at the shelter where she worked. She had a British accent, though it was a while before the kitten learned what that meant. The lady came from some place a long, long way off, but a lot of people there like cats and taught the little girl Alice how to care for them. The long-haired black cat she named Knasher because he knashed his teeth. Now spelling is a foreign concept to a cat who mostly meows or sometimes purrs. She heard Ms. Marcy say, "We would have called it gnashing, but it comes out about the same." He preens his silken fur with his rough tongue. MoneyPenny wondered if longhair cats have rougher tongues because they need to groom and smooth and separate their thick coats.

Anyway, after several phone calls, one afternoon Ms. Marcy opened the front door and a dark-haired lady bustled in with two cat carriers and a bag of cat food. It seems we should not change the food too suddenly for fear of upsetting someone's delicate tummy.

Ms. Marcy petted MoneyPenny and said aloud, "Now my darling girl, this is your choice. I will always love you. If you want to share that with the boy cats, they can stay, but if you are afraid of them, they do not have to stay here." She petted MoneyPenny in that special place under her chin and rubbed her face along the kitten's stripes.

The kitten had almost become a grown cat now. She understood what a serious decision she had to make. As the boys peaked from their carriers, she heard their thoughts:

"What if she says, No? The shelter is crowded and noisy and a bit scary." Here, flashes of lots of cats on catbeds in cages with kibble bowls flitted into MoneyPenny's vision. She had her own bed in most rooms and slept on the softest cushion on the couch in the living room. The short-haired boy was a tabby sort of like her, taller and darker colored. He projected insecurity as he slipped around behind his sturdier brother to look at her.

He didn't look dangerous. What if she let them stay and then they liked to pounce on her? She could tell each of the fellows was bigger and stronger than she. About that time, Knasher snorted and green snot flew out of his nose. He hurried to clean it up as if apologizing. She cringed at the yucky stuff, but he was so quick, she had to giggle a little. I guess it wouldn't be nice to make fun of the poor guy.

She forgot he could hear her. He wiped his face with a speedy swipe of his paw. "I can't help it. Had the problem as long as I can remember. I'll try to keep it cleaned up."

The tabby said, "I'm Manny, and we've been together from the womb. You get used to it, and he is really warm to sleep with on a cold night." MoneyPenny didn't know what to say. She never thought of sleeping with a cat. She slept on Ms. Marcy's bed just by the pillow.

As the boys explored, MoneyPenny followed them around, trying to feel what they felt. Ms. Alice and Ms. Marcy spoke in whispers, so MoneyPenny just read their thoughts. Ms. Alice was so hopeful and so worried that the boys would be accepted. Mom was excited too. It seemed she had a long-haired black cat for most of her adult life until a couple of years ago. Memories of a tornado of a cat named Chispa and a dignified girl named of all things, Goodgirl flew through Mom's mind for MoneyPenny to read. *What if I let them stay and they steal her heart?* The thought terrified the tawny girl. *She promised she'd always love me.*

Mom must've felt her kitten's concern. She picked up the little girl. "Here is what you have to understand. Love is not measured like a can of cat food that could run out. It flows like a stream that comes from the sky and never runs out, but refreshes all it contacts. A mother loves each of her children in different ways according to their needs. There will never be another MoneyPenny nor another Chispa. The love for you did not end the love for her. But because you can share love for the boys, they will share back." She rubbed the fur down the middle of MoneyPenny's back and MoneyPenny felt her body rumble in that vibration she was learning to call a purr. At that point, Knasher looked up and they all heard his firm humming purr.

Did he say, "Please keep us!"?

Mom put MoneyPenny on the floor. "Hoot, hoot," Knasher commented.

Manny protects his older brother Knasher
and meows for them both.

Manny said plainly, "Meow! I do the meowing for him."

The tawny tabby girl tiptoed to each of the boys, lifted her face, and touched her nose to each boy. "OK, you can stay," she thought to each, and Ms. Marcy heard her.

When Ms. Alice carried the empty cat carriers out to her car, MoneyPenny thought she saw a tiny angel in the back of one. As the car door closed, he waved to her.

"So, Little Darlin'," her dark angel friend said to her after all this time, "You got your task done. We angels have decided to award you a pair of wings. I think you need to visit with some of the birds outside to learn to use them. The trouble is, if you go flying around, people are going to be scared and think they are going crazy. So, we are going to have to figure a way to camouflage the wings whenever you are out. I don't know what your foster bros are going to think about them, but you can work that out yourself." He gently took her into his robe pocket and being old enough to enjoy an easier way to climb stairs, he whispered a prayer:

"Lift me, Lord, to Thee!"

Whoosh, they were on the highest step before the Gates. The big silver angel held out his hand again. This time, she nearly filled his hand and the calluses no longer tickled.

He held a pair of wings hinged like a bat's strong wings. But they shone with tawny tabby stripes to match her fur. He laid them ever so gently on her shoulders and his fingertips smoothed the edges into her fur. "There, MoneyPenny, you are cat number eight in the newly devised phalanx of Angel Cats. Combining the virtues of the kindest people and the smartest cats to help people and cats in need." He stretched her new wings behind her. They felt lighter than she had thought they would. She flexed each one to try them.

"Don't you go pulling an Icarus on us. You better get that crow that caws in the back yard to show you how they work. Just because you are an angel does not mean you cannot be hurt." He folded the wings one at a time and fitted one on each side into that groove where the fat pouch hangs on a cat. She had never thought about getting hurt. She always sort of feared the raucous crows in the back yard. Now she was apparently expected to trust one of them to teach her to fly.

"C'mon, Little Darlin'." her dark angel protector said, picking her up. And whoosh, they were standing on Ms. Marcy's deck looking into the backyard where a few crows picked at corn on the ground."

"Who was Icarus?" she asked.

"He was a boy who got wings and was too big for his britches. You better go back to being our little MoneyPenny. Don't you show off those wings yet, even to Ms. Marcy."

"What are they for, then?" she asked.

"You will know when the time comes." He said as he disappeared.

CHAPTER 3

MAGIC CAT LEARNS TO FLY

The talented tabby girl cat looked in wonder at the Dark Angel with the shabby robe. He held a pair of wings over her head. "Be still, Little Darlin'. Gotta get these fitted just right so you can use 'em, and you can hide them."

She twitched her fur over her shoulders, excited but a little scared.

"You're fine, now. Close your eyes."

She felt insecure with eyes closed. As a predator, a cat depends a lot on sight. She closed them for her favorite angel. To her surprise, she quit worrying as she trusted him to take care of her. She felt his warm fingers search through her fur. How light the wings felt.

As if to answer her question, he murmured, "Archangel Michael supervises making of wings for our new cadre of Magic Cats. The frames are hollow, like bird wing bones. The skin is smooth and thin like expensive material, covered in fine short fur and colored to match the cat receiving the wings."

She felt him rubbing something into her skin right behind her shoulder blades.

"OK, Little Darling, open your eyes now. You have to learn how to open and close them, then how to lift and lower like the flaps on an airplane," he said as he supported her body with a finger. He gently pulled the left wing away from her body. Almost as a reflex, she pulled it back. "Good Girl."

He did the same with the right wing, and again, she pulled it back. "Good, that reflex will get them folded safely against your body. Now, let's lift both as if to take off." She thought about lifting her shoulders. "Atta Girl."

She saw the edge of the left wing by cutting her eyes left and checked the right one the same way. "OK, you've watched birds fly." Think what it must feel like to flap your wings.

She tried to imagine being a bird. She couldn't flap her elbows the way a person could. She sat on her haunches and lifted her front legs. She saw the wings flap forward and then upward so she could hardly see them. "Good Girl, now pull down hard." She tried to follow his instructions and felt herself lifted almost off her feet.

After a few more attempts, she actually lifted up. She was excited, but exhausted.

"OK, you need to rest. The next thing you have to learn is how to hide them. We don't want to scare folks with a flying cat. The wings are designed to fold into the loose skin just above your fat pouch." His gentle fingers massaged the spot to make her aware of where to aim them. She tried to think and feel with her shoulders how she could scratch an itch just where he had rubbed. She felt something wasn't quite right.

"Here you go, turn your head and use your mouth to settle them here at first." She felt like it was sort of cheating, but a lot easier with her tongue in grooming mode. Sure enough, the fur had stripes that blended right into her tawny, tabby stripes. She began to wonder how she could get home from the Rainbow Bridge, realizing she would never make it with her new wings, and it was a long way to travel on foot.

"We will carry you this time. When we get you home, you can take lessons from those crows in your back yard." She cringed. She had always feared those great black birds. They were as big as she, some even bigger. How could she trust them?

"ArchAngel will send some of his neophyte cherubim to instruct the crows to help you," Dark Angel assured her as he picked her up and held her inside his angel robe. This flight would be her first time in his arms. She felt safe but enjoyed hugging to his secure body. They sped back to earth and landed in her backyard. "I'll check on you in a few days to see how you are progressing. Probably best if you not brag to your lady just yet," advised Dark Angel in farewell.

MoneyPenny hated to lose her guardian so soon. She bent around and used her tongue to secure her wings to her body. She felt pleased at getting them disguised.

After an uneventful night, MoneyPenny woke to a perfect day and realized her dream of flying was coming true. As soon as Ms. Marcy left for the shelter, MoneyPenny scurried down the pine tree into the back yard. As if planned, a murder of crows fluttered and hopped around some roadkill they had dragged to a sunny spot at the edge of the road right by her yard.

Hesitantly, she approached the large birds. One with a spec of white on her chest cocked her head at an angle to stare at the cat, her golden eye glittering as she concentrated. "Caw, caw," she stated. Several crows made brief squawks in answer and turned toward them.

MoneyPenny faced them with concern as one of the smaller ones hopped toward her. She wondered if smaller meant younger in this strange new animal culture. Then she heard his thought. "Sissy face here must be the one our sponsors told us to look out for."

That gave her a shot of confidence. She could think to the crows to communicate. She felt they wanted to see what she already knew. She took a deep breath and spread her wings. Several birds leaned in to see her wings' material. She knew she had to stay confident in front of the group. After all, they outnumbered her.

"Looks like they will work," declared the first one to meet her. Are female crow hens? She thought. Her answer came as, close enough. That bird assumed the role of matriarch and mentor. She gestured with her beak to the youngest one to get him to come forward.

MoneyPenny sensed he was ready to demonstrate a stroke or two. She watched and tried to sense what he felt as he moved. She tried to imitate his move. It felt pretty good. After a few strokes, she felt the birds approved her work. The concern of the glossy black birds made the newest Angel Cat feel good about herself and amazed by their kindness. She knew they had been ordered to help her, but felt they gave genuine care with their instructions. The young bird and the senior hen shared joy at her progress. By the afternoon, she could fly up to the rail of Ms. Marcy's balcony and also launch herself from the rail.

Next day, Dark Angel came and congratulated her and her new feathered friends on their achievements. "Now, Little Darling, you have one warning from ArchAngel Michael: You must take every caution to keep people from seeing you. We just can't have people around here panicking over UFO's or fearing they are going crazy seeing a flying cat. It is your job to stay out of sight or high enough that they can't make out your shape. Get some practice now. I have a couple of new angels trying their guardian skills protecting you."

Encouraged by his approval, she took a deep breath, spread her wings, and lifted up. She tried to look out for branches as she flew between the trees. Fortunately, people seldom wandered down the lane this far. She gained confidence as she flew. She noticed a young crow flew nearby. She wasn't sure how she felt about the corvid guardianship now.

"Don't get your feathers fluffed, Sissy face. After today, you are on your own. I've got to learn new skills getting meat off bones and using pebbles to raise water level in small pools or dog bowls people leave out."

After a tiring day, she had all night to schmooze Ms. Marcy and worry about a solo flight tomorrow. Morning brought anticipation as she enjoyed her breakfast with Ms. Marcy and Dad. He watched the morning news on the television as they ate. She felt impatient for them to go to work and prowled around the room from one soft chair to the couch to an empty dining chair pushed under the table. The tablecloth hid her. She realized it could be an advantageous hiding place. A place if she ever needed it. Finally, she heard Mom calling her to say goodbye. She projected a reassuring thought to help speed her off to the shelter.

She slipped through her cat door onto the balcony, leaped onto the rail, and lifted off. She flew just above the trees and headed toward an open field. She glanced briefly for any people on ATV's or hiking. OK, all clear she told herself, and flew into the sunshine. It felt great. Maybe this feeling was an angel's reward for getting to heaven.

MoneyPenny got so comfortable as she felt the air currents and discovered ways to use them to carry her forward with little effort. She barely noticed that she drifted toward a farm with a neat house with green shutters and a large old barn with some kind of lean to attached.

Some birds about the size of crows walked around pecking the ground. From some TV commercial she remembered they are chickens. Several red ones seemed to stick together. A couple of white ones looked bigger as they pecked along the edge of the pen. Had someone scattered food for them? She wondered idly what chickens ate anyway. She heard a sound she recognized from dad's cell phone: "Cock-a-doodle-doo!" A larger chicken with a red blob on the top of his head and under his neck stood on the edge of a water trough. He had iridescent black and blue long curved tail feathers sort of like some on one of Ms. Marcy's hats. He tossed back his head and crowed again.

Motion on the porch caught the cat's attention. Light glinted off a pair of glasses on a white-haired old man who held a long stick of wood with a metal pipe sticking out. He pointed it up. She got so concerned, she almost forgot to keep flying.

A loud boom sounded followed immediately with a rattling of some gravel or sand landing around her. Her sensitive nose detected something smokey. Oh, why had she let him see her?

Had he shot at her? Why would he want to hurt her, and where could she escape? In terror she tried to swerve, but her skills hadn't reached to making quick, sharp turns. She felt herself sinking. All she could think to do was flap her wings to get lift. She did begin to rise, but not fast enough. Another shot came close with stray pellets peppering her tail. If she could talk, she would yell, "Help!"

Suddenly a breeze picked her up a bit and a mist filled the area, concealing the man. Two angels swept her away, and then they held her in front of Dark Angel.

He frowned. "What was your one rule from the ArchAngel?."

"Don't let people see me," she mewed.

"You forgot to look. That old farmer protected his chickens, granted not from a flying cat, but from the hawk he believed he saw. If the Guardians hadn't blown a mist over him, his next shot probably would have found its target."

That thought made her shudder, Could an Angel Cat be killed, or hurt the way some of the shelter cats had been hurt? She felt so stupid and so guilty.

She hated to disappoint her Dark Angel friend. Would he quit caring about her now? "I'm so sorry," she cried. "It was such a pretty day, and I just learned to use the thermals to climb. I looked each way when I started. I did," she declared. "Then, I guess I forgot."

"You can't forget again. Do you know how worried I was when the Guardians called me? You could have gotten yourself killed! How would that make Ms. Marcy feel? She loves you more than any cat she's ever had."

MoneyPenny wasn't sure what "killed" meant but realized it might cost one of her traditional nine lives. She sort of remembered she already lost one to a close call with a car before she went to the shelter and landed in PetCo. So, was she down to seven instead of nine?

"Do you understand now that what you do affects others? What would your getting seen and having people upset do to my reputation with ArchAngel Michael?" She never thought her doing something affected others. She sure didn't want to get her good friend in trouble. Who knew an angel could get in trouble? All she could do was apologize. In her saddest tone, she told Dark Angel, "I'm so sorry. I didn't mean to be selfish. I want to learn to use the wings for good."

"All right, Little Darling, we've all had a scare. Yes, it's your fault, but since you had a life to spare, we can go forward. The Guardians blurred the man's memory a bit, making sure he remembered a red hawk after his chickens. At least he won't be telling his Sunday School friends he shot at a flying cat. You are now on probation as an Angel Cat. You need to help someone pretty soon to recover your good reputation.

The sassy young crow showed off but she learned a lot.

CHAPTER 4
A PURPOSE IN LIFE

MoneyPenny the cat angel shrugged her wings, looked carefully for witnesses, and flew from the grass in the yard to a chair on Ms. Marcy's deck. Not too bad, she thought, glad to be past the rough first flights.

"Good job, Little Darling!" The friendly dark angel with his shabby robe startled the tawny tabby girl.

"Where did you come from?"

"I've been visiting with some of the silver seraphim's. We are proud you've learned to use your wings and that you have been cautious about letting any people see you. Now that you are a full-fledged angel (pun intended), we think you need to find your purpose in life."

"I thought my purpose was to keep Mom happy and help the rescued boy cats to feel secure. Ms. Marcy loves petting us and brushing us and giving us treats, too."

"That is all fine. But you have earned special powers to do more to help the lost or hungry cats of your land and the lonely people, whether children or oldsters. Even with the cadre of Angel Cats expanding to ten, each one of you is needed to help."

"I'd like to help, but I don't know how."

"Open your hearing powers. I bet your Ms. Marcy worries about a lot of people, and you know Ms. Alice grieves when the shelter is over-crowded because then she might have to turn away a poor pet in need."

"Oh, yes, but I never thought what I could do."

"Suppose you get acquainted with some of the animals in need and see if one of them could be a companion for a lonely old person or a sick child."

"If I figure out a match, I could use my powers of suggestion to some people, and now I can fly to get close enough for the person to hear me."

"That's the trick, Little Darlin'!"

Ms. Marcy came out to the deck carrying a sack of birdseed. MoneyPenny followed her as she stepped carefully down the little stairway to the ground and poured feed into the feeder hanging from a nearby pine tree. Sure enough, the tabby heard her mom's worries about a group of cats needing a home. Their owner was very old and unable to care for them. In fact, the poor lady needed to leave her home of sixty years to live where people could bring her meals and keep her place clean for her.

MoneyPenny sat and curled her striped tail around her front feet. She wondered where she could go to find people who need a cat. Would she have to find a home to take all of them? Were they feral? She felt Ms. Marcy's thought picture of three kitties eating from bowls lined in front of a cabinet. OK, so they lived inside at least some of the time.

She heard the children chattering from the nearby schoolyard where they lined up to get on the school bus every afternoon. Maybe she could slip into the bus and listen to the kids. Surely a few of them were lonely and wanted a pet.

She carefully planned her flight to keep trees between her and the bus as close as she could. She was close enough to almost jump in. But the windows were closed. How could she get in? The driver pushed the lever to pop open the door and she saw the children crowd around the steps. She ran under the bus, hating the oily smell. She cringed at the thought of that gunk on her fur. She waited as the first kid, a dark-haired little boy, jumped onto the bus step. Glad he didn't land on me. Need a few kids for cover. The smaller they were, the noisier. Then she saw an older girl walking to the bus. As the girl stepped up, the cat slipped between her feet and under the shadow of her dragging book bag. When her unknowing hostess turned to get into a seat, MoneyPenny darted under the row of seats and leaned against the wall. She felt herself panting from the tension, her first flight in public, and her desperate dive to get aboard and find a hole to hide. She wondered if anyone would hear her catching her breath.

As the driver closed the door and started the bus, the children seemed to all talk at once. MoneyPenny thought it should be easy to eavesdrop thoughts. Until she found one thinking about a pet. Wrong. So many thoughts. Kids have busy lives to worry about: sports, all kinds of games and teams, and so many hobbies and collections, and Valentines. She had trouble separating the thoughts. Some little girls were hoping to get a Valentine from some boy. What was that? She tried her photo thought connection. A red and white or pink and white card with writing on it. Why would that be useful? They couldn't eat it.

Finally, from the back of the bus she felt a tremor of misery. A little boy projected waves of pain. His father was gone. MoneyPenny knew she would need Ms. Marcy's help to help him. So she would have to get off when he did to find where he lived to be able to fly home and show Mom how to find him. He seemed to be one of the last to leave the bus. The cat planned how to get ready to leave with the boy. She'd have to be quick. One of her talents, but she didn't want to get trapped under his feet. He was the boy who jumped on the first step. She hoped she could stay out of sight. The driver was too busy and concerned watching that the children got off safely to notice their feet. If a child saw her, probably no one would believe the story.

As the little boy exited, the cat spurted down behind him and dived under a hedge beside the sidewalk. She followed him and listened to his dreary thoughts: dreading an empty house, no tall dad to throw a ball any more or ask him about his day. Had the boy's dad gone to the Rainbow Bridge ahead of him? Even Ms. Marcy couldn't bring back his dad, but maybe a kitten would give him someone to play with and a job to do taking care of it. A sudden thought hit her: what if he were one of the boys she had heard of that took out their pain by tormenting cats? One sure way to find out. She trotted out of the hedge near the boy and flipped her whip-like tail in invitation, ready to flee if she felt danger.

For a few seconds, nothing. "Hey, Kitty. What's your name? Maybe I can guess."

MoneyPenny tried projecting her name as she turned around in front of him.

"Let's see, you are sort of brass colored. Brits call money brass. Are you Penny?"

She lifted her chin.

"Naw, pennies are copper, not brass. Can I hold you?" he asked, putting down his book bag. He reached for her, but she believed in hard to get as a lure. He took a piece of meat from a half-eaten sandwich from the lunch pack on his book bag. "It's pretty good. Mom made me a sardine sandwich for lunch," he said, holding it toward her. What cat's aloof to fish? She tiptoed to his hand. She snagged the meat with her paw, backed away a step, and sat to dine with a wrap of her tail over her front paws.

She projected a thought, "If you tell me what's wrong, you will feel better." She sensed his desire to hold her but couldn't risk getting captured. The boy took his book bag carrying it over one arm, doling out treats to MoneyPenny as he trudged up the sidewalk to his front porch. No mom waited to welcome him. He sat cross-legged by the door. "I know it's a little crazy to talk to a cat, but as long as the other kids don't find out, I'm OK." MoneyPenny moved close enough to get petted. He stroked her head and rubbed down her back. "You're soft. I wish I could keep you as a present for my mom. She's awful sad with Daddy gone. He's dead. A drunk driver creamed his car." The tabby rubbed the back of her head on his hand. She would need Mom to help with this. She purred an experimental rumble. "Hey, you're purring. That means you like me, doesn't it?" She blinked at the dark-haired boy, then leaped up to the railing.

"Please don't go. Wait till Mommy gets here. She might let me feed you."

She needed to get home to think-talk with Mom. She bounded off under the hedge until near enough to some trees to stretch wings and fly home without attracting attention.

Mom was just getting cat food ready for them as she dived in the cat door. She began thoughts remembering her day, not the part with her angel friend, but the boy and his need for a kitty. Mom called Ms. Alice. They had a lot yet to solve. Mom had never explained to Ms. Alice how MoneyPenny communicated to her. And she would need to find out who the boy was and whether he could even have a cat. She wasn't sure if her senior lady wanted to send the three cats together.

The angel cat's photo projection memory helped Ms. Marcy figure the street and number where the boy lived. That helped. Ms. Alice had a friend who worked at the school who found out the name of a dark-haired boy who had recently lost his dad in a car wreck. Mom asked if her friend could let the youngest cat, still a kitten, go by herself. The old lady thought the kitten would like a child because the kitten is a boy and likes to play. They got the mom's name and called.

As soon as the lady determined they were not trying to sell her anything or beg for a donation, she let Ms. Alice explain about the kitten needing a home.

Here, Kitty, I wish you could stay.

CHAPTER 5

THE ANGEL CAT MEETS HER FIRST DOG

MoneyPenny seldom got a chance to stretch her angel wings and just fly. This Sunday she felt free as she lifted into the treetops where, if some human glimpsed her, the person would probably assume a hawk soared amongst the leaves. Her wings matched her tawny tabby stripes, almost the coloring of one of the smaller Texas hawks. She had made a habit of checking the ground often in case she spotted someone in need.

She found a perch to sit comfortably in a tall pecan tree for a while. Being an Angel Cat could be tiring work as she ran errands for her angel friends and used her telepathic powers to offer guidance to humans who were about to take unfavorable risks. She could think, "What do you think God would want you to do?" or maybe advise as the Dark angel suggested, "Can't you find a kinder way to tell your friend what he needs to hear?"

Sitting up on the sturdiest of the high branches, she had a good view of the leaf covered ground and felt a slight breeze on this hot Texas afternoon. She took a deep breath. Mom, Ms. Marcy, volunteered on Sundays at the animal shelter where workers were overwhelmed. As school started, many parents no longer wanted the pets they had bought or adopted to entertain their kids during the summer vacation. Some respectfully brought the animals to the shelter and left an appropriate donation. But many just dropped them over the fence late at night for the workers to care for in the morning. Ms. Marcy worried that they might be hurt falling, or some bigger ones might attack the smaller ones.

As MoneyPenny glanced down, she saw movement. Did the pile of rags blow in the wind? Not wind, she decided. She squinted and made out the outline of an animal. Something felt very wrong. She floated to the branch closest to the creature. She heard raspy breathing and a tiny whimper. This was too big for a puppy. The Angel Cat focused on asking it what was wrong. "So tired. Ran all I could. No food. No person helped."

"Are you a dog?" she asked.

"English setter," whispered from the rags. Tan specs dotted the once white fur. MoneyPenny dropped to the ground beside the ailing dog, tucking her wings under her stripes as she landed. She touched her pink nose to the dog's nose and nearly gagged on the awful breath. She was too far from the shelter to think a message to Mom. She smelled blood on the dog's paws. "Let me make these better," she thought. She licked a few swipes of her rough tongue over the pads on the left forepaw. She knew her saliva had healing antibiotics. She suspended her sense of smell and taste so she could get into the grimey spots in the grooves of the little bitch's feet. At first, she flinched and once whimpered.

MoneyPenny had heard Mom say that dogs would clean up each other's vomit. She decided to try something. She had just had a nice long gulp of water before getting in the tree.

I know I can't carry water to her. So, she burped some liquid into the corner of the slack mouth. When the dog turned her tongue into the drops, it was nearly white from dehydration. The patient had no energy to lift her head, but the cat sensed her gratitude.

"Trust me. I can bring my mom back to help you. She will bring water and food and a blanket to carry you."

"Too bad I can't carry a cell phone," thought MoneyPenny. But she landed on the kitchen windowsill and slipped inside. Ms. Marcy had the next best thing— speed dial on her phone. The Angel Cat's paw tapped the number 6 and connected to Mom's cell phone. She couldn't talk in words, but she projected the image of the dog and her cut paws. Her heart cried out her despair and need for help. She heard Mom tell one of the other volunteers she would need supplies to rescue a dog suffering heat exhaustion. Ms. Marcy kept her cell phone on her bluetooth headphone and the women hurried out to the car. MoneyPenny projected pictures of the route she would have flown from the shelter. Ms. Marcy kept very quiet.

"How do you know, Marcy, where it is?"

"Don't worry, my GPS will keep me straight."

As soon as MoneyPenny was sure Mom had all the images she needed to find them, she flew back to the dog. It was almost rush hour, so she had to be careful to stay out of sight. She shuddered to recall the time the dark angel saved her when a chicken farmer mistook her for a hawk when she was first learning to fly. Her danger today came from the hoards of children leaving school and bus stops. The youngest did not know a flying cat was impossible, so might claim to see her. As she flew, she hummed a kitty tune of meows, "Please, please, don't tell the Grownups on me. Please meow the Grownups away. Please meow them astray." Once at least, she saw a child point to the sky, then quickly hold his hand over his mouth.

At last, she spied Mom's car easing into the woods near the dog. She was pretty sure Mom had figured out her special powers since she had earned her wings, but she didn't want to scare the bejeezus out of the lady with her. She checked for leafy cover as she floated down behind the big old tree. Its bark was rough and covered in lichen. It made a lot of shade to protect the dog.

As the women got out of the car, the frail dog tried to stand to flee. MoneyPenny projected to her, "Rest easy! Friends! My mom will help you."

Uncertainly, the dog recalled some people throwing rocks as she struggled.

"It's OK. I promise. They can take you to the vet's office. He's really nice."

Mom's gentle touch at last settled the setter. Mom's friend, Ms. Vikki, was one of MoneyPenny's favorites of the shelter ladies. She took a cloth from a cooler and wrung it out to place it over the dog's face. Mom put the head in her lap and used her finger to open the mouth just a bit. Ms. Vikki held a squirt bottle of fitness water and dripped some into the mouth. The dog mustered enough strength to lick her lips. About then, she formed a terrified thought. "You're a cat! I always thought I was supposed to chase you."

"After the vet cares for you, maybe we can play."

"My goodness gracious, Marcy, how did MoneyPenny get here?"

"I must've left the kitchen window open. She gets around whenever she thinks she can help another animal. Last week, she opened a gate so some dairy cows near us could get to their water. The neighbor was sick, and his friend didn't think to check the troughs."

MoneyPenny peered at the poor creature.

CHAPTER 6

HELPING A FRIEND

MoneyPenny settled on the balcony where her friend Snowflake lived and tucked her magic wings under her tabby stripes. She mewed softly, but her friend did not appear behind the curtain as she usually did. Snowflake's mom was at work, where could her little friend be? She was never allowed outside. MoneyPenny hopped up to the ledge on the bathroom window. Maybe she could be in her litter box. "Meow," said MoneyPenny. No answer. She climbed down the trellis to check the kitchen. Snowflake was not a greedy kitten, but she occasionally slipped downstairs for a snack of the special kibbles her mom got for her. No luck. The graceful tabby Angel Cat turned away, discouraged. She didn't have a phone to call the vet's office.

Maybe one of her angel friends could help her find her friend. She had a scary thought. Could something bad have happened? Could Snowflake be at the Rainbow Bridge? As soon as MoneyPenny got amongst the trees, she opened her wings and flew around behind the hill to the backdoor of one of the churches where she often met her angel friends to check for any assignments. She saw her friend the dark toned angel with the soft voice. He held out his hand to her. "Hey, Little Darlin'!" he said.

"Can you give me a pass to the Rainbow Bridge?"

"MoneyPenny, it's not your time to go yet. You can't just drop by for a visit."

"What's the matter?" he asked in concern.

"I can't find Snowflake. I'm worried something has happened."

"Her little owner, Christina, would be upset. Maybe you can find her now that school is out. Maybe she is at the library using the computer."

"Good idea. If I can find her coming or going, she will pick me up and pet me. She always likes to rub the stripe down my back to make me purr." MoneyPenny left in two powerful strokes of her striped wings.

Sure enough, she found the little blue eyed girl. The tabby felt the girl's sadness and fear. The young teen buried her face in the tabby fur, tears soaking the cat in her arms. She coughed as she sobbed that Snowflake lay at the vet's, Much of her gorgeous white fur had been burned off. She had deep burns on her skin. When MoneyPenny projected her question, Christina's tone became angry. "I found the story on FaceBook. Tommy Longdon was laughing about the flames from his dad's gas can for the lawn mower burning so fast as he threw his dad's lighter at the gas he poured on the cat. Tommy was mad because his dad died, and his mom told him to mow the yard."

MoneyPenny wondered, "What can you do?"

"I can teach him a lesson he will never forget."

The teen's answer worried the tabby cat. She feared the child would do something so dangerous she could get arrested or start a fire. She licked the girl's hand and stared at her. "I know which way he goes home. I can get some rope from Mom's barn and I know where my dad used to keep his lighters and lighter fluid. I can get a bunch of his old handkerchiefs Mom hasn't given away yet."

MoneyPenny projected all the calming thoughts she could muster.

"I don't care what happens to me. Anyone who owns a cat will want to reward me, not punish me. Tommy is not the only kid who has lost a dad."

The cat could not picture the nice little girl overpowering the teenage boy and dragging him somewhere to use the flames to get even. When Christina set her down, she did not bound away but just hid in the flower garden to follow her home and wait.

As promised, Christina came out of her garage with a couple of lead ropes over her shoulder and a lot of handkerchiefs sticking out of her pockets. In a grey Walmart sack MoneyPenny could see a can of lighter fluid and some small plastic tubes. Those must be the disposable lighters. She looked around slowly, as if checking for any grown-up who might stop her. The tabby scooted from shrub to shrub following the girl with the determined stride. Soon they entered the woods at the edge of the neighborhood. The path must be the schoolkids' shortcut home.

Christina bent over to stash the bag of supplies under a wild tree growing by the path. She grabbed the trunk of a big old tree and reached for the first branch. With little effort, she lifted herself until she perched above some clumps of leaves. Then they waited. MoneyPenny concentrated on calm thoughts of Christina's mom. The lady often visited Ms. Marcy. She was a teacher at the high school. The cat considered flying home to get Mom to help. Before she could find a safe spot to take off, she heard footsteps, muted as if sneakers worn by someone lightweight. She peered from her shrub to see the boy with his forelock in his eyes. He muttered as if his anger choked him. The sensitive angel cat felt the boy's frustration and fear, anger overwhelming his grief.

Christina leaped from the tree onto Tommy's shoulders, wrapping the leadropes around him. The startled boy struggled, but she shoved a handkerchief into his mouth and forced his hands together. Despite his shoving, the little blonde fastened a ziptie around his wrists. Then she stood up and pulled him up too. "You are not the only one to have a bad thing happen to your family," she declared. "But the rest of us prayed or cried. We didn't take it out on an innocent animal. You are about to feel what you did to Snowflake. Maybe it will be a preview of your time in Hell."

"She was just a cat," complained the boy.

"That is the worst thing you could say. She is my cat, my friend, my baby. If she dies and I'm able, I may come back and kill you."

MoneyPenny had never seen a child as angry as Christina. Tommy was impressed too. His fear had a sweet scent to it. He tried to get loose to run. Christina kicked him back down, aiming between his legs. She dragged several handkerchiefs from her pockets and pulled the lighter fluid from the bag, flipping the top to pour it onto the handkerchiefs. MoneyPenny hated that smell. It reminded her of the worm and flea prevention they put between her shoulder blades every month or so. Then the girl started to stuff the soaked handkerchiefs into the boy's pockets, shirt and jeans, back ones too!

Terrified herself, MoneyPenny jumped behind the tree, ready to fly home for help. Despite Tommy's struggles, the girl held a lighter in each hand and started several miniature fires. Tommy screamed. "That is how Snowflake felt. She is still at the vet's and may not live. You better hope she does."

At that point, they could smell flesh burning. "Please, make it stop!" Tommy begged.

"Remember Snowflake."

MoneyPenny projected to Christina her guilt. "He is a person. You cannot do this. You will be in so much trouble. Your mom didn't teach you to do something like this!"

"I don't care what happens to me. I don't want to go on without Snowflake." But as she sobbed, she grabbed a half gallon of water she had hidden in the sack with the lighters. She started to pour it on the little fires slowly burning through the boy's clothes. Blotting a towel over the wounds, she snipped the zipties and ran, yelling over her shoulder, "You deserve worse. I hope you go to Hell when you die."

As MoneyPenny lifted airborne, she saw the boy stumbling to his feet heading into the neighborhood. She flew so fast, she forgot to look out for observers. She landed on Mom's balcony right outside their kitchen window. Mom looked up before she could stow her wings under her stripes.

"MoneyPenny? What on earth?"

The telepathic cat did not bother with words. She projected images of Christina and Tommy. "Get Snowflake's mom as fast as you can," she projected, then sent an image of the shortcut through the woods. Of course, Mom got on her cell phone and called Christina's mom.

"Milly, it's Marcy. You need to get out here. Fast. We need to help Christina."

MoneyPenny didn't bother to eavesdrop on the rest of the conversation, sure Mom could get help in motion. As an afterthought, she added the possibility of an ambulance for the boy Tommy Longdon.

Of course, Tommy told his mommy that the crazy girl attacked him for no reason. Mrs. Longdon called the sheriff. When he came to Christina's house, the defiant girl screamed, "I want to file charges against the Longdon boy for animal cruelty! I want to go on trial. As long as the jury owns cats, I'll never be punished." She turned on the recording she had pulled from FaceBook of Tommy laughing about the cat's fur burning.

"What a mess," the sheriff said with a shake of his head. He sounds like that actor on "In the Heat of the Night," thought the cat. To Ms. Marcy, the cat projected, "What kind of mother doesn't know when her kid is in the kind of pain that he would do such a thing?"

As the video came to the part where the teenager showed his victim in flames, the senior officer turned grey. Mrs. Longdon cried, holding her son to her.

"All you cared about was the yard getting mowed for the people coming to the wake," Tommy groaned.

Through her tears, she said, "Son, I thought you would want to make Dad proud of his yard. I thought you wanted to help, you are not a child any more."

The boy stood with his clean shirt hanging open and his pants loose at the waist to prevent irritating his burns under their light bandages. "Aren't you going to charge her with anything?" he asked, Pointing at Christina.

Ms. Marcy said, "I don't think cruelty to animals fits. Damage to your clothes? Maybe you could put the story on Facebook? But they probably shut down your account for the cruelty video."

Christina's mom, Mrs. Murphy, said, "By the way, Sheriff Hodges, I want to file for the vet bill on Snowflake. How much depends on when she can come home."

"You have to do that in civil court, not the Sheriff's department. I think all of you have health insurance through the school system, so don't get into shoving that back and forth." He wiped his face with a large white handkerchief. It sent her a whiff of JuicyFruit gum. MoneyPenny almost felt sorry for the old guy.

For the first time in a couple of hours, she wanted Mom to call the vet about her friend Snowflake. She shuddered as she cleaned the last of the hated lighter fluid from her front paw. To her surprise, the deputy came in the room with a phone in hand. "Sheriff, I got that vet on the line for you."

MoneyPenny could hear the scratchy voice of their vet, Dr. Russ. She let out a sigh she hadn't known she held in. Snowflake could come home tomorrow. Maybe Mrs. Murphy would let her visit. She had a lot to tell the little kitty and wanted to let her tell her story too.

Snowflake's burns healed just in time.

CHAPTER 7

CAN AN ANGEL CAT GO TO A CAT SHOW?

MoneyPenny felt so pleased with the praise she got from Ms. Marcy after guiding her to rescue the dog, an English setter. But after a week and the dog beginning to recover and gain weight, no one was talking about that adventure any more.

Then Ms. Marcy came in with a flyer she found at the shelter. "Big Cat Show! It had a date on it. That didn't mean much to the cat, who had never heard of a cat show. Mom and Snowflake's mom chatted on the phone, so of course MoneyPenny listened in.

"Do we have to join The International Cat Association to take a cat to the show?" asked Ms. Millie.

"No, we can see if the cat wins any points and if we want the points to count, we can join before the show year ends, whenever that is. But," Ms. Marcy added, "it's only $15 to enter. They don't have to have papers, either. The association wants to encourage people to adopt cats and then show them, so they have a special division called 'Household Pets.'"

"What do they have to do?" MoneyPenny heard through the phone.

Mom said, "they don't have to do anything special, but they have to seem like a good pet, sweet, and fun. And I guess they shouldn't bite or scratch any of the judges."

"Our cats could do that!" came from the phone.

After a while, MoneyPenny felt sure Mom and Ms. Millie were planning to take her and Snowflake, her good friend. She knew that Snow had never been to a show, so she would not know what it was like either. MoneyPenny wracked her brain. Who could she ask? She remembered a gorgeous tabby Maine Coon who lived in a mansion at the end of their lane. His owner was a society lady who dressed a bit fancy and had parties. She put on a party with gambling to benefit the shelter and celebrate the championship achievement of Tabby McForest.

MoneyPenny was not particularly impressed, but had heard he would always show "Champion" in front of his name. She stretched, from her neck to her shoulders and through her back to the tip of her whip-like tail, wriggling her stripes. Since learning to fly, she had dropped in on Tabby at his safety enclosed balcony. He didn't care about his title, but said the party was fun, and people fed him treats. He was even allowed some intimacy with a lovely buff colored Maine Coon lady. He said there might be a party to welcome their kittens later.

She slipped out the kitchen window and carefully spread wings to fly to see Snowflake.

Her lovely little friend had almost recovered from her terrible burns. Her silken white coat was coming in, though still a bit thin. "Have you heard what our moms are planning for us?" MoneyPenny asked.

"Not exactly. Figured something was up when Mom came in and examined my coat so carefully. She mentioned I need my nails trimmed. Not sure I want that."

"It can't be too bad, if our moms want it done to us."

"I guess, but why??"

"Bet it has something to do with the Cat Show."

"Whaaat?"

"They found a written ad for this event for cats in about a month. It's at Town Center. I can't figure out what it will be like. I don't think we have to prance around a ring the way the horses do at one of their shows."

"What if we don't like it?"

"You know we will still be nice because we love our moms and want to please them."

"How can we find out more about it?"

"I'm going to go ask Tabby, that big Maine Coon down the road."

"Can you take me with you?"

Try as she might, MoneyPenny could not think of a way to get Snowflake to the mansion down the street. "Maybe I can give Mom the idea for Ms. Millie and her to take us to see Mrs. Society. I don't know her name. I promise I'll try, and I'll tell you everything Tabby thinks we need to know."

"Thanks, MoneyPenny. Don't get too tired running down the street."

"I won't," she promised as she slid off the balcony into the tree beside it.

She looked carefully for anyone who might be startled to see her before she leapt into the air and flapped her wings. In no time she found the tall pine tree beside the McForest balcony. She couldn't see Tabby anywhere, but the balcony was still the best place to gain access to the house. Since it was a warm summer night, the sliding door stood open. After securing each wing into the groove beside her fat pouch on each side, she ducked through the door and under the edge of the white silk drapery. The gold woven cord distracted her as she batted it around for a minute. It was so pretty and shiny! What girl doesn't like bling!

Suddenly, the huge resident cat landed beside her with a little chirp, sort of like a cardinal's sound. "Oh, Tabby," she said with a mew of admiration. His fur was so rich and soft and thick and long.

"What are you doing here, little Tabby girl?" he cooed.

"Tabby, we need your help little Snowflake and I."

"My owner done gave money to the shelter to help with that little white cat's vet bills."

"I know. It was very nice, but we need some information from you."

"From me?"

"Yes. We figure if you went to enough shows to become a champion, you must have found a way to enjoy them. We are afraid our owners are planning to take us to a show next month. What is it like? What do we have to do?"

"Well, I'm in Championship rings, so I don't have to do anything except not run off and not bite or scratch. But you are House cats. The shows call it Household Pets. They don't care about how close you come to a breed standard because you may be mixed breeds."

"So do we have to learn tricks?"

"Not really. Most rings have a cat pole you can climb if you want to. They kind of like for you to play with a toy or purr and rub on the judge."

"But what's it like?"

"Hmm, guess I haven't thought about it much. Mom started taking me when I was just a kitten. I just wanted to be with her. She took my bed and put it in a wire crate there. She draped curtains all around it and left an opening so I could see out. I had some toys and water and kibbles, too. Then an announcement sounded about championship longhairs and she'd take me in her arms and hurry to a ring where 10 or 12 cages, smaller than the one my bed filled, formed a line on tables around the area. She found one with a blue card (I'm a boy and boys get blue) and my number for the day, and gently pushed me into that little door. In a while, a person I didn't know came, lifted me out, and set me on the center table. Sometimes the person would play a minute, but mainly checked flexion of my joints. Studied my head, fluffed up my tail and my mane, and tried to get me to 'talk.'"

"What do you mean, talk?"

"Well, I guess you've noticed that we Maine Coons don't meow much. They'd like to hear some sound we make. Like this," He added and let out a rolling little howl I never heard a cat make before," MoneyPenny later told Snowflake.

"The best I could figure from what he thinks he saw in our pet rings, they don't care about our joints or head shape, but our ears have to be clean and our nails clipped. His nails were clipped the day before a show. And, get this, we have to have a bath with vinegar in the rinse to be sure all the soap is out of our fur. They may play with us with a toy or try to lure us to climb the pole. And he said the worst thing about a show is how noisy it gets."

So during the visit to report to Snowflake, MoneyPenny asked, "What do you think?"

"I don't know. I want to please Mom. She does give me treats and pets all the hard to reach places. I think she really is proud of me, especially since my junior mistress got in trouble trying to get even with the boy who hurt me. Maybe it would be OK, something different."

So the two cats agreed to cooperate with whatever their owners decided.

MoneyPenny was beginning to get excited, and when she saw her friend the Dark Angel a few days later, she told him as much as she could recall of Tabby McForest's information.

"But, Little Darlin',"he said, "when that judge person goes to handling you, as expert as they are on cat anatomy, then he's sure to find your wings. At best he might think you have some weird growth. No tellin' what else he might wonder about. You gotta find a way out without tellin' yore lady why."

MoneyPenny hated to admit how disappointed she was. And she hated to upset Mom. What could she do? If she played sick, Mom would be worried and take her to the vet and learn she wasn't sick.

About then, a nice young woman stopped by. She introduced herself: "I'm the social worker with the case of Christina, the girl who burned holes in the pockets of Tommy Longdon to get even for his burning her kitty. My regular job is substitute teaching, to pay for my graduate classes. I see you are the counselor assigned to the case. I hope we can talk about Christina."

Something she said got MoneyPenny's attention. She knew substitute teachers taught a class when the regular teacher could not come. What if she could find a substitute cat to go in her place? She liked the idea. Surely her telepathic powers could help Ms. Marcy believe that she thought of the idea on her own. Now. Who could go from our family? Mom once referred to Manny, the shorthair tabby cat with the charming green eyes, as, "My middle child." What did that mean? MoneyPenny had no idea.

She approached Manny. "How would you like to go somewhere special and do a favor for me and for Mom?"

"Huh? What do you mean?"

"Let's go in the kitchen and figure," she said, hoping Mom would be serving the guest a snack or cup of cocoa.

Reluctantly, Manny rose from the bed he chose and followed MoneyPenny. Still grateful that she had accepted him to the family, he hoped to see a. reason to help her out. When they got to the bottom of the stairs, they smelled cocoa and cinnamon. "Never know what they like about that stuff," he thought in pure cat.

"Oh, Manny,Dear!"exclaimed Mom, leaning past a coffee table to stroke his stripes as he purred.

Mom turned to the young teacher. "He's like a middle child." The girl looked puzzled.

"He got adopted into our family. His minutes older litter brother has striking long fur in rich, blue-black. And Money Penney, his foster sis there, is so sweet and smart that eveyone talks about her. So Manny invented tricks to gain attention and petting." She turned toward them. "Here, Manny." She patted her hand on the table.

Manny looked at MoneyPenny. "Think I should go?"

"Good idea." She sent the thought.

He hopped to where Mom's hand rested. He sat a second, then looked up at Mom.

She said, "go on, sweet fellow, show off. After a second, Manny flopped onto his side, exposing his stomach's extra soft fur. He wriggled just a tad, achieving his desired effect. Miss Russel touched her fingers into his fur and he felt warmth with a light scratch on his tummy. He resisted the urge to kick.

"Ooh, my, I think he likes it. He's purring."

"Yes, that is one of his tricks," Mom said as she lifted him and set him on the bar. She kept a hand at either end of him for a moment to let him know to stay. MoneyPenny thought she knew what comes next. Mom leaned close to her tabby boy. The cat stretched his neck up so his forehead bumped Mom's.

"How darling!"

"He will give you the best kitty eskimo kiss ever if you lean over here." Mom pointed.

Miss Russel leaned down and Manny bumped his damp kitty nose right into hers. "Oh, I could fall in love!"

MoneyPenny shrugged her shoulders as she thought to Mom, "Manny could be even better than MoneyPenny as a Household Pet." From Mom's thoughtful expression, it looked like one problem was solved.

Maine Coon Champion knew a lot about Cat Shows.

CHAPTER 8

FRIENDS TRY TO SHOW

MoneyPenny hoped her friends could relax and have fun at the cat show their loving owners got so excited about. The Friday came and several of the volunteers from the shelter drove up to help bathe and groom cats. One girl was a gentle expert with the nail clipping tool called a guillotine. Another pair of girls soaped the cats with a special cat shampoo Ph balanced for them. They had a large pitcher of water to pour for rinse. MoneyPenny smelled something like salad dressing. She heard the girls, Sally and Jean, chatting about a cup of vinegar, apple cider vinegar, rinsing all the soap out so the cats' coats would shine and feel like silk. The only part the cats objected to was getting their ears cleaned. Mom and Ms. Millie used cotton swabs with some oil. Its pungent aroma stung the cats' noses, and they anticipated the treatment would hurt, tensing themselves all over. MoneyPenny tried to broadcast calm thoughts to convince her friends their owners would not hurt them. "Close your mouth so you won't accidentally bite Mom. It's OK. It can't last but a second."

She had to concentrate to avoid struggling from her own twinge of fear. As the warm, dry towels wrapped the cats, they realized the shelter girls had brought four of the shelter cats in carriers. They all smelled faintly of lavender and maybe a hint of peppermint. MoneyPenny knew these were calming therapy. She did begin to relax and chatted with Manny and SnowFlake.

They did feel clean and pampered. Cats being natural opportunists, all of them tried mewing and begging for treats to celebrate this special occasion. The shelter cats stayed in Mom's enclosed porch under the balcony. Ms. Millie took SnowFlake home for the night. MoneyPenny and Manny got to run free with Knasher and eat in their own bowls and sleep in Ms. Marcy's bed as usual.

That was reassuring, though she saw Mom put a favorite bed for each of them in the car with a huge bag of supplies—little litter boxes and bags of litter. The best thing was that toys and treats filled a fair sized bag.

Morning came early, but the car ride was blessedly short. Mom left the "kids" in the car while she carried all the stuff in. The cats missed all the fun of mom and Millie and the girls setting up their own cats' crates with beds and curtains and litter boxes and water bottles.

When the ladies carried their darlings into the big convention center, the air hummed with so many people, cats and scents of cat food, fresh Kitty litter, and hurrying people.

A nice lady showed Mom where their first ring would be and showed her how to spot her cats' numbers on the cages. For a little while, people seemed to be, for the most part, catching their breaths. The loudspeaker came on with a welcome from the show secretary, the person who knew where everything was and how to succeed. They played the national anthem. The house cats recognized the song from having heard it on TV, but the shelter cats were on high alert from the confusion of sounds and smells. They didn't exactly know they were there to find forever homes. MoneyPenny sent helpful thoughts to them across the room. She had never imagined such activity.

Finally, Mom wrapped Manny in a towel and hurried off to the ring for short-haired Household Pets. I could peek through the curtains of my crate's drapes Mom fixed. It looked pretty much as Tabby McForest described. I could see Mom putting Manny into an empty crate with a blue number above it. I projected to him as hard as I could, "You sure look great up there. Just relax into the hands of the person who picks you up. You're fine!"

I could tell he was still tense. It was pretty noisy all right. Mom spotted a front row seat. A strange lady who seemed nice, leaned over and spoke to her. I couldn't hear what she said, but could read Mom's reaction. She relaxed a little and thanked her new friend.

I projected to Manny, "Everything is fine. Mom is making a new friend. It's good you are not first so you can see what the others do for a little while." Mostly at home, Manny and I just communicated the way all cats do, with an occasional meow or sniff and body language. It took him a minute to realize where the ideas came from. He looked off out of the cage, more or less toward our little camp. My mind shouted to him, "Right you are! Just relax! It's almost your turn. Remember your best tricks to make friends: offering tummy rubs, giving gentle head butts, and if you can reach, your Eskimo kisses. You can do it! Make a new friend!"

The man was definitely a cat person. He sensed Manny was new and nervous. I couldn't hear what he said, but it was kind, I could tell by his body language and the care he took to lift Manny out and set him on the table. He had a cute little bird with real feathers on a string attached to a small stick like a miniature fishing pole. Manny waggled his quick paw at the "birdie." The man let him loose, but kept his hands ready in case of any panic.

"Relax," my mind yelled. "Tummy rub! Tummy rub!"

Manny sort of flopped onto his side. The judge seemed to appreciate that and gently touched the striped cat's soft belly fur. I could see Manny tense.

"Don't kick. Relax! Relax!" I wanted so much to be next to him as we were when the postman came in sometimes. He didn't kick. Inspired, I projected in my happiest mental voice, "Remember our nice postman, how you made friends."

I guess that did the trick. When Manny relaxed, the judge man smiled and gently lifted him back to his numbered crate. I saw Mom smile and the lady beside her did too.

When the judge finished looking at all the waiting cats, the clerk at the center desk stood and sent everyone back to their home crates. Mom was clearly confused. She leaned toward her new friend. As they approached, carrying their tabbies, I could hear her explaining the finalist numbers would be posted. It seems there were even more household pets for him to look at. We waited, SnowFlake and Knasher are longhairs, so they had a turn now.

As Mom put Manny in his cage to take Knasher out, our triumphant tabby purred protectively, "it's a cinch! You two will wow them."

Neither of our darlings seemed too happy, but both lay snuggled in their blankets in their moms' arms. At least they would be crated near each other. Show protocol called for alternating boy/girl for safety, so they happened to be next to each other. Knasher took over as protector of SnowFlake. Three other black cats and two other white ones occupied some of the cages. I saw a tabby Maine Coon that looked a lot like Tabby McForest. I thought out to him, "What are you doing here? These are Household Pets."

To my amazement, he answered., "I got lost from my owners, and my papers were gone by the time I was picked up. The Shelter took me in. Course, I couldn't explain my daddy was a famous Champion named Tabby McForest.

Sometimes I see a Maine Coon at a show and send him a message, but never know if he thinks I died in the cold."

"What's your name?"

"Kind of complicated. My birth name was Greenfield's McForestson. The Shelter called me Tabby. My new lady calls me Tab Hunter after an actor she loved from afar as a teenager. I try to purr a lot for her. Figure it is the least way I can thank her for taking me home."

"Your dad lives near us. He helped coach us to get ready for this show. I can go tell him we found you."

I got so busy with Tabby's son, I forgot to watch our kids. Mom and Ms. Millie came back with them in their arms. Then we all got a couple of Temptations treats. I like trying to make it fall in my mouth without even touching it. "Numbers are up in Ring Six!" called the friendly lady from up the aisle.

Mom dashed toward the ring where our kids had been. She practically danced back toward us. "All three numbers sit in the slot at the tops of three crates. We need to carry them down there." She grabbed a blanket from our pile of stuff and handed it to Ms. Millie for SnowFlake. She pulled out the one for Knasher and reached for him, cooing, "Good boy. Good Boy!"

In a minute she came back for Manny. I kinda felt left out. I wonder if Mom knew how much my coaching helped calm our lovely cats. The friendly lady was back, congratulating Mom and Ms. Millie. While they were learning the custom of taking only the plastic ticket off the top of the flat ribbon and putting it on something called a Rosette, I sort of paced around in my cage. I had plenty of time to figure how to open it without even using any angel skills. I heard the judge tell his little volunteer helper to bring three of the club rosettes from the box at the front desk. "Our new exhibitors didn't know they were to have one for each cat. Then he said, "You're all fixed up; you're ready with a ticket for your placing in household pet and as second best long hair black. Then you took the second best long hair white" he said, turning to Ms. Millie "And you get a ribbon with a ticket for second best tabby shorthair. Out of six that's something for a new exhibitor!" He ended petting Manny a little extra.

Suddenly the PA system blared, "Cat Out. Cat Out. Shutdown. Shut DOWN."

Even I could tell that could be a disaster for a scared kitten or an older cat dragged to a first show. My smart paw slipped the latch on my cage and I was out. I hurried a loud thought to Mom that I was going to help, "Don't worry!" I ran under the tables of cages. Like a neighborhood of alleys for my use. As I went, I tried to pick up catspeak for information. An older lady had stumbled trying to carry her cat in her arms. He was a tabby Maine Coon. Could that be Tab Hunter? He hadn't said it was his first show. Maybe it was just her first show. The bad thing was, she was headed to the bathroom to do some last minute cleanup on his ears. That was outside the back door. If he got outside, would the lure of the street draw him away from the hall's inside confusion? Would he even know where his home crate waited for him?

Tab hadn't told me anything negative about his new lady nor how long he had been in the Shelter before she adopted him. People were yelling about checking the parking lot. That just made it harder for me to sneak out to look for him. I projected a thought to him that I could help him. "Just think to me where you are." I concentrated as hard as I could and reminded him I was the little Tabby girl who knows his daddy. Finally, I heard his thought come with his little chirp and trill.

"I didn't mean to make her trip. I'm really sorry. I only shifted a little bit. She didn't use her walker."

"But Where are you?"

"I'm near a bathroom door, I think."

"Stay there. I know the way back. I'll be right there."

Just as I was scooting behind someone going out, a man spotted me. "Here he is!" The man screamed and slammed the door.

What kind of cat person couldn't tell a small pet tabby girl from a champion quality Maine Coon male! Now how could I get out? Meanwhile, I ducked behind some bleachers shoved against the wall in the dark. People came from everywhere to help catch me, calling out to each other, shoes squeaking on concrete.

I tried sending false thought messages that I was somewhere else, but that didn't seem to work any more. Finally, I called to Mom where I was and why using our thought speak secret way. By that time, she had our boys put in their crates and Ms. Millie had SnowFlake cozy and comfortable.

I was breathing hard, as if I'd flown miles. I still cowered behind the bleacher in the dark. Mom finally caught on to just think what she thought I should do to help.

OK, I knew where Tab Hunter hid. So far, the people were missing the prize. I wanted to take Mom there. I told her so. She seemed to want to help the poor cat. He hadn't been to a show in a few years, but he remembered enough to know he didn't have to panic. I just didn't want us to get grabbed by some hero-seeking maniac." Please, Mom, come get us," I projected.

"OK," I heard her answer. I settled into a blanket on the floor and looked toward her. She and Dad stood together. That was a surprise. He didn't usually come to our activities.

I stalked my way over to the outside door. I crouched and waited for Mom.

I heard her voice in my head, telling me she would help. I felt so much better. "Are you here yet?"

"I'm sorry I couldn't walk faster. If your friend really wants to we can take him and his person and you, for a little while, home. His lady is a little old, and had a pretty bad spill, but she is better and stronger. I can bring her to see your friend, too."

I considered and waited. Soon, Mom was nearly asleep. I wondered if Dad could hear me. I never tried to talk to him before, but he was strong, and might be able to carry us out somewhere. "Mom," I thought, "wake up. How did you get so sleepy? Can you bring Dad to help carry us?"

"Sorry MoneyPenny. Don't know what happened."

I could tell she was close.

"Get Dad to open the door, and I can run through to take you to Tab Hunter."

So she asked, and Dad opened, and I sprinted through and climbed as high as I could on a fence. I sensed Tab right below me. Then I saw him and showed Mom my visual image.

She cooed to Tab. He seemed happy to hear her. Dad leaned down and lifted the heavy striped cat with his long fur and perched him on his shoulder. Tab seemed fine with Dad's handling. I almost wished he lifted me too. Mom opened the door, and Dad carried Tab. Then Mom picked me up and wrapped my soft blanket around me. A man met them at the door when they came through. He seemed glad to see the lost cat.

After that, the day went on as Dad took Tab back to his mom. She was planning to leave because she got tired but was so glad to see her beautiful boy who trilled a greeting to her.

Mom explained that we knew her cat's sire and his family. She lived in a small town nearby, so was anxious to meet them.

Ms. Millie came looking for Mom. "We're up in Ring One. Come on. I took Manny for you." Of course, we were back in the show mode, and she got Knasher ready while Ms. Millie fluffed SnowFlake's lovely white coat.

Now that the kids are happy enough with the show, I bet we have to come back. Mom and Ms. Millie sure do like the look of those rosettes with all the tickets stuck on them. Wonder if I had come by myself, if anyone would have found my wings. Guess Dark Angel was right, though. Sure would mess things up if they found my wings on the judging table.

Mom and Miss Millie liked the TICA ribbons.

CHAPTER 9

MAGIC CAT MEETS A BARN CAT

One spring day, MoneyPenny looked out to one of God's most beautiful mornings. Chirping birds almost drove her crazy, but she could tell the air currents of the breeze would make for thrilling flight. Maybe she could fly down the lane toward the estate where Tabby McForest lives. The trees along the way smelled so fresh and the shade would make protection for her secret. The lawn at the mansion reminded her of a rainbow of colors. She landed on the rail around Tabby's luxurious "catio," with its potted trees inside and pot plants of mint and even some catnip. His large Maine Coon body sprawled over a cat-size chaise lounge. He trilled a greeting.

"Welcome, show girl. I can't get out of here. I slipped out when I was a kitten, and Mom flew around the yard in frantic worry looking for me. She called a contractor and ordered this place built right away so I'm happy enough inside."

MoneyPenny said, "I forget how lucky I am that Mom trusts me to come outside."

"By the way, did your son's mom ever get to meet you?" she added.

"Yes. She's a nice old soul. I think my son has a good home. Mom loved explaining to her all about us Maine Coons. She asked a lot about us and what we need."

"I'd like to see him again, too. But now," she changed the subject to her mission, what is that place next to your back field where the buildings are and those humongus dogs?

Tabby laughed. "Those aren't dogs! They are horses. Completely different. They carry people around on their backs."

"Why would they ever want to do that?"

"I don't know. I guess you could go down there and ask Bright Eyes, their barn cat. She isn't much use. Can't catch mice. She's about to lose her job if she can't figure that out soon."

"Why should she catch mice?"

"That's why people with barns keep cats around, to prevent mice from eating up the grain they buy to feed the horses."

"Is Bright Eyes nice? I think it'd be fun to talk to her"

"She's nice, just not very brave. She hasn't come up here. Go see her, and come tell me about it. She is a silver mackerel tabby with huge green eyes. As far as I know, she is the only cat there"

With that suggestion from Tabby McForest, MoneyPenny checked for observers and flew through the trees to get the protection of the shade and camouflage. She saw the building that must be a stable or barn. She landed on the roof and tiptoed to a large open window and leaned in. She saw a lot of big oblongs of packed grass. The room smelled lovely.

She crawled in the window and across the hay bales. "Bright Eyes?" she called with a gentle meow. No answer. The metal roof cooling sounded like a fairy's tinny trumpet's tentative tinkle. She crept through a narrow space to the opening to the stairs down from the loft. Under the stairs, she saw a pile of gunny sacks. She floated down the stairs to investigate. She heard a fierce growl like a very large dog and spun around.

Under the step, she spotted a pair of bright green eyes. "if you're Bright Eyes, Tabby, your neighbor cat, sent me to meet you."

"OK, I'm Bright Eyes. I"ve got enough to worry about without entertaining McForest's friends."

"I'm MoneyPenny. I live way up toward the city street in the house with the second floor balcony on the back."

"I haven't gone very far that way." Her little mew sounded timid to MoneyPenny.

"Sorry you have a problem. Maybe I can help. Want to tell me about it?"

Bright Eyes crept closer and swiped her face with her paw. "Our barn manager says if I can't start killing mice, I will have to go to the shelter. I don't want to go there."

"It's not so bad. My Mom volunteers there. But maybe I can show you how to kill mice, and you won't have to go. Your kitty mom should have taught you."

"I was almost old enough for my first lesson when she disappeared. The lady that rides here says a coyote probably got her. Then the rider lady took me and my brother inside and fed us for a long while. My brother came from a Siamese daddy, so someone wanted him right away."

"Well, my kitty mom taught me how to hunt, but I haven't practiced much because Mom doesn't seem to have mice. I haven't heard any. Can you hear them here in the barn?"

"Sometimes. I almost caught one, but it bit my paw. I licked that wound for weeks to get it well. I can usually find one in the Shetland pony's stall. She's not very aggressive."

MoneyPenny recalled the thrill of the pounce and neck grab. Maybe she needed a toy mouse to demonstrate for Bright Eyes. "Do you have any toys? Especially toy mice?" she asked.

"They don't want me to play."

"That could be a problem. I'll be back. I gotta go home and get a toy mouse."

"When will you be back? You're my only hope." The young cat's meow came as a series of high-pitched mews. Her forehead's black M furrowed into three crinkled lines.

"Can't be sure when, but I will try to hurry."

The little grey striped girl thought she saw a tawny hawk flit through the trees across the paddock. It must've been something; the horses stopped grazing to look. They are her friends. One horse stomped a rat with his hoof and showed it to her so she could drag it over to the feed room and get credit.

MoneyPenny lifted up to the balcony by the kitchen. She was glad to project an image of Bright Eyes to Mom.

"Hi, MoneyPenny. Where'd you find your new friend?"

She sent an image of the stable so Mom would know. "She's just barely a cat, but the manager wants her to kill mice to earn her keep. I think he cheats on her food to keep her hungry, saying, 'She can eat mice.' She needs me to teach her how to hunt. I need to take some of my toy mice to show her how to grab."

Mom began to worry. "Cats need to be fed well to hunt for sport. If he wants to get rid of her, you need to make sure he knows where our shelter is."

"Meantime, keep me posted how she progresses with the lessons." Mom came out on the balcony and opened the fancy kitty tote devoted to MoneyPenny's sweaters, an extra bed, and over a dozen cat toys, several of which had rat bodies, sometimes with fur, sometimes with feathers, in all colors. Ms. Marcy sniffed the mice to find the ones with catnip. "Here, sweet girl, These three ought to be enough for now. If you need more, I can refresh the others later."

She put them in a plastic store bag so MoneyPenny could get her paw hooked in the loop while she flew.

This time, Bright Eyes came when MoneyPenny called her name. As the magic cat unwrapped the toy mice, she said, "Now don't expect real mice to smell of catnip." She took the largest mouse with its fur cover and placed it on the stair step. Bright Eyes approached with her head up.

"How am I supposed to catch it?"

"Here, behind the skull, is where you need to get your teeth, crosswise, like this," she said and demonstrated. Through a mouthful of fur, she mumbled, "get your top eyeteeth on one side of the spinal cord and bottom ones on the other side. You should be strong enough to break it when you jerk up. Here, try grabbing."

She drew back to leave room for the grey striped girl.

"Which side?"

MoneyPenny wanted to laugh at the dumb question. Instead, she tried reassuring the youngster: "It doesn't matter. After you've done it a few times, one side will feel easier to you."

"OK, here goes," she said, though far from sure. She stepped up to the toy, leaned over, opened her mouth as wide as she could, and grabbed where her new friend pointed.

"Quick, jerk up. That helps snap the cord."

Bright Eyes jerked her head up. The toy mouse hung from her fangs, limp.

"Good girl!" MoneyPenny was surprised how good it felt to see her student succeed. "Now, come from a couple of steps up. Run to it and grab it away from my paw." She sat, poised to yank the mouse forward.

When the grey girl leapt, she was surprised as the mouse slid forward. She fought to adjust her leap. "Darn! What'd you do that for?"

"A mouse will seldom lie still for you to bite him. Now this time, I'll pull the mouse so it will give you some challenge." She set up the toy on a bale, so the cat had to leap up.

This time, Bright Eyes took careful aim and came at a run. Her tutor reeled the toy along the path. Bright Eyes leapt and jerked the mouse all in one move.

"Good Girl! You got him! I'll leave the toys so you can practice tonight. Tomorrow we can hunt up some live ones," MoneyPenny promised.

The next day, MoneyPenny caught one of the live mice to demo to Bright Eyes. Both cats breathed with quick short pants. They put their trophy by the feed bin where the manager would see it. They checked around, listening. They heard faint scrabbling behind the stall wall. MoneyPenny dropped a stone behind the inner wall to flush a mouse. It worked. A mouse scooted out the end. Bright Eyes darted after it but could not pounce, and grab so she tried to grab with her paws. She lifted it to jerk it, but it wriggled from her grip and escaped to slip under the wall.

"OK, that means you need to read what your wrist whiskers are telling you. They are called propillae. You have two or three growing from the insides of both your front paws the spot people call your wrist. These specialized whiskers are very sensitive. God gave them to us to let us know how good a grip we have on our prey. In a few grabs, you will understand."

Just then, they heard heavy footsteps. Bright Eyes dodged.

So MoneyPenny did the same. The heavy boots belonged to Ben, the manager. They heard him shout from the feed room, "Hey, Abbey, your useless cat may be learning something. Come look!" eey ey AssHe.

"He must've found your mouse," MoneyPenny whispered in her softest kitty voice. "You need to keep practicing on the live ones. After a while, the others may leave. That will make hunting harder if you have to get them in from the field. I hope your people will reward you with a better supper."

The magic cat slunk around to hide in a stall behind the feed room where she could project her idea to the two people.

In a few minutes, the man called, "Here, Cat, you can have some kibbles."

Bright Eyes started toward him, but not as fast as anyone would expect. Then the lady said, "Her name is Bright Eyes. Here, Bright Eyes," she called, leaning over with a can of cat food in one hand.

Bright Eyes the Barn Cat finally learned to Catch Mice.

CHAPTER 10

MONEYPENNY PLAYS COMPUTER WHIZ

MoneyPenny woke one morning surprised to see Mom already sitting at her desk. That lighted screen thing stood open before her. The tabby girl rubbed against her mom hinting for breakfast. "Darn it! Leave me alone. I've got to get this order finished and print a brochure for the shelter. This stupid machine has given me fits." When the cat stretched to see over the desk, she realized by the state of the coffee cup with pile of napkins nearby, Mom must've worked all night.

About then, Dad strolled in. "What's going on, Dear?" "Oh, "Roger, I'm so frustrated. I have to get this brochure to the printer. We are planning an Open House at the Shelter to raise funds, and I've got all the pictures of adoptable animals to put into the brochure we are putting in all the petfood stores and vets' offices. I just have to get it right, and I can't get the formatting tools to work right."

MoneyPenny felt her person's tension. She tried to use her best stress relief tool, her purr. She rubbed her body fur on Mom's bare leg, purring as loud as she knew how, which wasn't very loud, but Mom felt the vibration. Her lady ran her hand over the tabby girl. "Thanks, Sweet One, I'll take a break and feed you right now in a minute." MoneyPenny puzzled how in a minute could be right now.

Dad leaned over Ms. Marcy's shoulder to stare at the screen. "First, Select All and Copy and Save," he said. "That way you won't lose what you have. Let's go through your options along the top to look for Page layout." He clicked a few keys. "Damn! Where is it? It's a basic procedure to get ready to print."

MoneyPenny got bored, she remembered she might have left some late night kibbles in her bowl, and padded into the kitchen feeding station. Her bowl was empty. "All right, Boys," she called, "Come help me get Mom in here to open our feed sack!" Manny and Knasher strolled in stretching from their long naps from one catbed to another. The lanky boy tabby sprinted into Mom's office and hopped onto the desk. "No! Manny, no!" Mom exclaimed. "Don't you dare touch the keyboard. No telling what you could mess up." All the cats wondered how just trotting across the keys could harm Mom's page.

Soon, Ms. Marcy did get up and put out canned food and kibbles for the three cats, always feeling good when she heard her darlings' happy slurping and crunching, so aware how some cats had no homes.

She fried bacon and eggs for Dad. All the cats' noses twitched in hope at the scent of bacon. They knew she'd never let them have a bite on the table, but a strategic purr or meew might solicit a tidbit for all under the table. Mmm, anticipation was half the fun, along with the crunchy salty taste. MoneyPenny hoped her mom felt better and solved her computer problem. "How hard is figuring out the computer?" she mused. "Mom's pretty smart, for a human."

As soon as Dad and Mom left, MoneyPenny hopped to the balcony rail and looked carefully to make sure no neighbors strolled about. She flew to the back door of the nearest church where she could usually find Dark Angel. As she approached, she scanned the few spirits gathered, some new folks, must've come to the Pearly Gates over the weekend. Sometimes the speeches folks gave at their memorial services floated around them. The Cat Angel guessed that was to encourage them as they adjusted to eternal life. She sat on her haunches and waited, looking forward to seeing the shabby robe of Dark Angel. This time, as he floated toward her, she recognized some of the ragged patches showed recent mending, no longer noticeable. Had he been promoted?

"Dark Angel," she mewed respectfully after he spoke to several of the new spirits, "When you have time, can I share a problem?"

"I hope your mouth works to share, the question is , 'May I?'" he teased.

MoneyPenny thought the distinction trivial but decided she probably shouldn't say that. "Yes, may I?"

"You know I'm glad to help if I can. Let me help those two souls huddled over there," he said, pointing.

"Thanks," she mewed and slipped over to a comfortable branch to perch and wait.

MoneyPenny projected her complex concern for her person to save the trouble of mewing out so many details.

"Little Darlin', that is strictly an earthly problem. I am no computer technician. Not atall. Now that doesn't mean, as smart and magic a cat as you are, that you need to be messin' with your lady's computer. Those things have a little Devil's dust about them. You be careful, you hear?"

"I'll be careful," she promised, disappointed and a little confused.

That night, Mom went to bed early, tired from her loss of sleep last night. Fresh from a catnap, MoneyPenny purred Mom to sleep and slipped off the bed and into the office. She leapt to the desk and stood over the computer. Mom remembered to close it. Darn!

Ever resourceful, the girl tabby sniffed all the way around the laptop's edge. From the scent of Mom's hands on one side, she decided that must be where she had to prize it open. Perhaps from her many activities climbing trees and sometimes screen doors and an occasional chair, she had good strength in her paws. She flexed her claws as far out as possible. It took her several attempts at different angles before she felt her claws on her right paw sink into the thin space under the computer's lid. She worked and wriggled until she had her right front paw all the way into the space and tightened her whole front leg to lift the lid.

"Whew!" she wheezed. She waited for the screen to light. After several seconds, she felt confused. Did she do something wrong? "Don't think so." She searched memory banks of all the times she had watched Mom work at the computer. Did she point somewhere? The cat concentrated on the keyboard, then realized the thing Mom typed on was separate, connected with a cord. The computer had its own keyboard.

She went along the top row with her nose. At the very edge was a small black square, slightly indented like a fingerprint, and it had strong scent of Mom's skin. She put a tentative paw on it. Nothing happened, but she sensed a slight warmth. With a deep breath, she pushed hard and soon a little apple lit up on the screen and a line started to move under it. She jerked her paw away. Soon the whole thing lighted up. Some words and icons showed along the top.

What was I thinking? She chastised herself. I can't read much. Only a few words. She did know to start on the left. She saw an icon she had seen on Mom's packages, a long curved arrow. She touched it on the screen. Pictures came up. Had Mom been shopping for catfood? She recognized a picture of their favorite dental treats. She tapped it with her paw. The screen blinked. She tapped it again and another picture appeared, a fancy water fountain that would let water bubble. Looked like fun. A tiny picture in red looked like a cart she saw Mom use at the grocery store. Would all this come to Mom or to the shelter?

She stretched thoughtfully, front paws out, back arced up, tail out.

What should she do? She watched some lists slide down with a few words and numbers on each line. A neat Red triangle had a word in it. OK, she touched it. The page disappeared and a different page flashed up. She couldn't see anything she recognized.

Knasher hissed from the doorway, "What are you doing?"

"Nothing really. Just like the warm feeling when it's on. Too bad we can't put it in one of our beds at night."

"You're going to get in trouble."

"Aw, Brother, don't be such a scaredy," Manny huffed.

MoneyPenny tried touching the button that turned the thing on to turn it off. She felt a bit proud of herself when the light went out.

"Come on, guys. We have a few kibbles we can scarf up before bed," she projected to the boys. They scampered to the kitchen and crunched a few kernels of choice catfood. The boy cats went to the cat beds along the wall by the fireplace, taking turns pawing a cushion to check for just the nicest puffiness. MoneyPenny hopped onto the foot of Mom and Dad's bed. She didn't want to wake them as she stepped between them and burrowed into a fleece coverlet left just for her.

That morning, Mom mumbled some surprise at the screen her computer opened to. MoneyPenny slunk out of sight behind the couch to wait. "Who knows what goes on in the minds of computers?" Mom mumbled to herself; or maybe she only thought it, and MoneyPenny's telepathy picked it up. Late afternoon next day, a delivery arrived on the front porch. Peeking between the curtains, the tabby girl identified the symbol she'd seen on the screen.

Mom puzzled over the order. "Could it be for the shelter?" She did not unpack the treats. Darn! Then she found the fountain. Apparently her curiosity won out to test it. She set it up in a corner of the large kitchen. The three cats came to check it out. Knasher drank with fast flicking tongue, slapping droplets out of the bowl. Manny put his paw into the gentle bubbles. He jerked it back, then held it. "It tickles," he discovered, with a cat version of a giggle. MoneyPenny feigned sophistication as she took a few dainty sips. The water did taste fresh and cool. She felt relieved to see Mom smiling while she watched her crew of cats enjoying the new equipment.

Of course, all this meant several phone calls for Mom to begin to worry if her computer had been hacked. The cats had no idea what that meant. One morning, she packed the computer and its mouse and cords into her soft case and toted it out to the car. From what she told Dad that night, the Geek Squad seemed confident her identity and credit had not suffered. However, her ego sure did. At one point, she even considered Dad might have played a prank on her to make her more cautious about leaving her computer unlocked. He reacted to the accusation with indignation.

MoneyPenny hadn't seen Dark Angel all week, so finally flew over to check in. "Little Darlin'," he said, you need to get back to helping other animals or some folks.

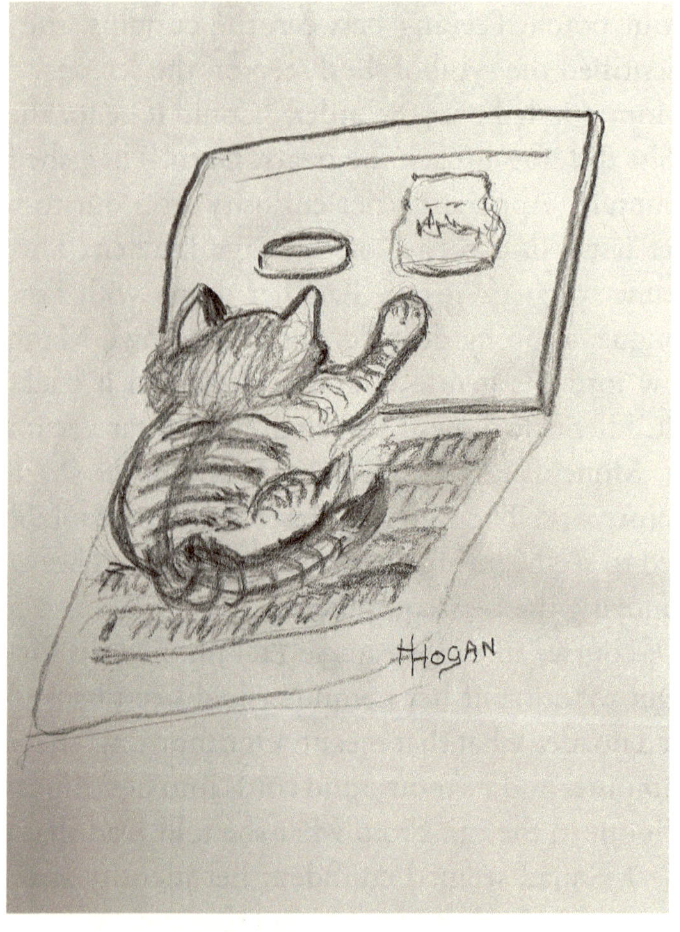

MoneyPenny figured this computer
stuff couldn't be too hard.

GHOST HORSE REVELATIONS

Ghost Horse Revelations

MoneyPenny stretched and decided this wonderful fall morning would be a great day to explore. The fall leaves would make great cover for her flight. She could start at the Rainbow Bridge with permission from Dark Angel. She could usually find him behind the nearby church with his new angels where he started their training. She flew through the trees to the edge of the woods, then flexed her wings, grown strong from practice. She soared higher, thrilled by her newly learned skill. When she climbed high enough that any human who chanced to see the motion in the sky would never be able to recognize a flying Angel Cat, but just glimpse a spec up above. Reaching the church, she settled softly into a bush near the back door.

"Morning, Little Darlin'," Dark Angel said as he sensed her arrival. "What are you up to today? Are you ready to rise and shine and give God the Glory?"

His question confused her. She knew people sang hymns to praise Him, but she couldn't sing, unless a mew or a purr counted.

"You are part of His glory with your powers and your job to help people and animals find comfort."

"In that case, yes, I'm ready. May I start at the Rainbow Bridge? I thought I could help spirits there find their family."

"Sounds like a useful purpose." He stroked her golden tabby fur. "You will know the way and pass without any obstruction. Have a safe venture and remember your purpose."

"Thank you, Dark Angel," she projected to him. She tried to remember the manners her mama cat had taught her and those she learned from Ms. Marcy, her people mom.

She flew high into a cloud and drifted a short while like a rudderless boat. Some sense told her to stoop down. Sure, enough the cloud opened to green fields marked with clear streams. In the distance, a rainbow quivered and shimmered. She took a deep breath. Below her wandered several hundred animals, mostly pets. She listened with her special sense to pick up their emotions. Some had clearly waited a long time, hoping their owner would come for them when his or her earthy time ended. Some seemed patient, but a few emitted an aura of discouragement. "Even if she remembers to come for us, I hear she is only allowed to take her favorite into Heaven with her. I always thought I was her favorite, but she had cats for most of her life. What if one of the earlier ones is really her favorite, or the one she got after I died?"

MoneyPenny got a lump in her throat listening to the sad kitty, apparently a beautiful Maine Coon. Surely, she reasoned, the father planned other rewards for the loving cats who could not be chosen. She planned to ask Dark Angel. The more she worried about it, the more she wanted to talk to the pets down there. As she drifted near the Bridge, she made out a large herd of horses. Those large animals that were not huge dogs. She wondered if she could understand horse speak. Her answer came with a cacophony of images as the horses remembered trainers and riders and lesson kids who fed them from their own lunches. It had never occurred to the young cat that other animals loved their kind owners.

A small, attractive white horse seemed to be right in front of her. He projected his thoughts as ideas rather than as nickers or whinneys. "I'm Cyrk, short for Cyrkumstance. My breeder couldn't afford to keep me because she knew I was not a perfect specimen of the Arabian breed that she could sell for a lot of money. She gave me to a nice lady named Floreen. She wasn't a trainer, not even an experienced rider, but she had a friend who seemed to know a lot, and they worked with me all summer. I learned to carry her at all three gaits.

"One cold day, I got in the trailer with another horse, and we went to a parade. Mom got all dressed up. My job was to walk beside the other horse who pulled a carriage. A lot of Mom's friends I met that day got all excited because we helped the group win some sort of prize."

"For several years, Mom brought me feed and sometimes brushed me, but didn't have time to ride. I wondered if I did anything wrong. I hadn't bucked or reared and certainly never bit anyone. Sometimes Mom held onto my neck and made sad noises into my mane. I felt warm moisture on my neck. Then one late afternoon the other lady came with a trailer and Mom led me in. I thought I was supposed to turn around, but the other lady explained I needed to stay at the front. We moved to a new stable. I had a new stall and made new friends. I had a good life. Mom even started riding me again. I began to ache in my joints. Sometimes it got pretty bad. Eventually, one night our kind vet brought the release we sometimes need, and I woke up here. I hope Mom will come for me someday."

MoneyPenny hoped so too. She wondered how long animals had to wait. Did cats recycle through kittens until they used all their nine lives? How would they know which owner to wait for or if they would follow into Heaven.

"We're not cats. But I don't know if Mom bought a new horse to replace me. What if she likes him better?"

The Angel Cat wanted to find out for the pretty white horse if he could expect his owner to come for him. Maybe she could fly home and get Mom to ask around. How many horse women in their area were named Floreen? Then she realized the animals at the Bridge came from all over, not just their neighborhood.

Suddenly, without any angel to project ideas to her, she felt memories flood into her mind. As if she had died, she remembered arriving and learning that all the horses enjoyed the Elysian Fields with rich green grass and clear cool streams to drink and to soothe their tired hooves. She felt her pads relax as if she had been a horse. So, if the owner could not take all his horses into Heaven, they still had their own heaven of good food and comfort with no pain and social life with no bullies. As a predator herself, MoneyPenny worked to imagine the built-in worries of prey animals. Life beyond fear made an extra benefit.

What would happen to her if Ms. Marcy were to take Knasher into Heaven to enjoy his luxurious warm fur? She remembered what Mom had told her when she let the boys move in: "Love is not a finite quantity like a can of tuna that can be used up. It renews and flows like a refreshing stream." In that case, was Heaven big enough for all of us? She realized that sounded impossible. Were there any other places for spirits of good animals? Which side of the Bridge should they be on? She studied the arched bridge with its shimmering colors. Animals seemed to come from one direction. Some of them looked a bit scruffy. They trudged onto the bridge. As they climbed up to the peak of its arch, their hides and fur began to lose the smudges and hair looked more vibrant. She figured the ones at the top felt better. Had their pain drained away? Answering her unasked question, the white horse said, "Yes, as we climbed, we got stronger and felt so much better, like having warm sunshine on a tired back. I guess we'd be crazy to complain about this place. Might be fun to have more children around with treats." The old fellow's eyes gained a spark of enthusiasm.

Even more than the population of horses, the dog category spilled across the grass, dogs of all sizes and descriptions lolled about, some stretched flat out, some curled up, some choosing shade, but more sprawled in sunshine, even exposing their bellies. MoneyPenny felt waves of anxiety flowing from a middle ized white dog with tan and red specks scattered in her long silken fur. Her head had a classic sporting look and her tail lay straight out behind her with long feathery tassels hanging straight off. The dog had clearly suffered. MoneyPenny thought telling her story might help the little bitch. She knelt beside her and stroked her with her tabby paw.

"I'm afraid my person will not come for me."

"Why not? Weren't you a good dog?"

"I nearly killed myself trying to be a good girl. I was so afraid of loud noises. One holiday, people around our yard kept lighting terrifying fireworks that lit up the sky. I just panicked and fought my way over the fence. I ran to escape the noise, but rain began with thunder and lightning. I ran through some shrubbery and into some woods. When I came out on a road, I couldn't see anything I recognized. I sort of stumbled along the edge of the pavement. I dived into the ditch whenever a car came by. Then a car stopped, and a lady got out. She sounded nice. When I lifted my head, she wrapped her arms around me, and half dragged me to the car. I didn't know what to do. She put me on the back seat, closed the door, jumped in the front passenger seat and said, "Hurry, dear, we need to get away from this neighborhood. I prayed to the great Canine that they would take me home. After a few days when they put me in a crate at night and tied me on a cable all day, I knew they did not want to return me to Mom and Dad. I didn't know how far they had driven us away from my home. I couldn't tell direction from inside the car. I just wanted to go home."

"How did you get away?" asked MoneyPenny. She casually nosed her fur over her folded wings.

"Whenever they tied me on a cable, I started chewing on it as soon as they left. It wore my teeth and tasted weird, but I worked on the same spot each day. I finally got through the plastic all around it and worked on the wire. Without its cover it got rusty. Pretty fast. I figured how to twist as I chewed and get it into my back teeth to gnaw harder. Finally, I got loose and climbed over the fence. I had trouble at first deciding which way to run. I just felt I should run south, maybe east too. Traffic scared me a lot at first. I didn't want to be close to expressways so sometimes I had to find a longer way, but cars and trucks weren't running so fast. I got awfully hungry. Trash cans could be a good source of food, but people threw rocks at me."

"How cruel." The Angel Cat felt sorry for the dog. Here at the Rainbow Bridge her paws had healed, and her body had a glow of health despite what had happened to her, "How did you come to be here?" MoneyPenny asked as she stroked the dog's silken fur over her shoulders.

"I finally began to smell a familiar pool scent like our neighbor's. I crawled into our driveway. I smelled my pointer buddy, Tuff and another female dog, not a setter. I was too exhausted to get to the door or even the gate into the backyard. It was just before dawn. Maybe I could last until the sun would warm me, and I'd feel better to bark for Mom or for Tuff."

"Is that what you did? Bark for help?"

"No. I'm not sure whether I fainted or just fell asleep. I heard Dad's voice say my name, Dottie. I could only open one eye part way. He dropped to his knees beside me and petted me. I whimpered to let him know I appreciated him. He got up, then leaned down and lifted me in his arms. He carried me inside and laid me on a soft hassock. He dried my fur with a towel and then spooned water into my mouth. I could barely swallow. He put a blanket over me. I felt better if numb."

"Did you have a people mom too?"

"I did, but she wasn't there. He used his fingers to poke a little canned food into my mouth. The phone rang. I was so happy to hear Mom's voice. He sounded so kind when he told her about finding me."

"Did she come home?"

"Next day, after he gave me food with his fingers again, Dad lifted me into the car and drove somewhere with noise overhead. He left me in the car with all windows half open. He dashed out and in a while I had no way to tell how long, he came back with Mom. She sat in the back with me and held my head in her lap. She talked that funny way folks do with kids and puppies. We went to our vet, Doctor R."

"What did he do for you?"

"He drew a little blood from my front leg and took X-rays of my body. He's tall but leaned down to stroke me."

"Although she is very thin, we're in luck that none of her organs have shut down. Give her a whole can of high protein/high fat dogfood every morning and a can full of kibbles wet with water and cooking oil every morning and night. I think we'll see her perk up pretty soon."

"I felt encouraged. We went home, and they fixed me a rich supper. I was so glad the kibbles were soaked because my teeth hurt too much to eat anything crunchy."

"That sounds good. How long did it take to recover?"

"I got stronger so that in a few days I could stand up to eat and drink on my own."

"But then a strange girl came to follow Mom around through all the feeding set up. She had stockpiles of food for all three of us dogs and three inside cats and four horses in the paddocks and barn. Mom explained that the old horse had poor teeth and had to have a lot of feed from her because he could not bite off and chew grass. The old cat needed wet kibbles and lots of canned food because she too could not chew anything crunchy just as I couldn't chew kibbles."

"All that required a professional pet sitter," MoneyPenny injected.

"I guess, I'm pretty sure they were paying the girl. Two days later, they drove away. I don't think they meant to abandon us. The girl came to stay in the house. She dumped kibbles in the feed bowls. I don't know what she did for the horses. I thought we could survive a few days and Mom would be OK. But a week went by. I was so tired. Another week passed, and I just lay around all the time. Sometimes we got kibbles in the morning, more usually at night. But they were always dry. If only she'd pour water on them so I could swallow them."

"Did they come home?"

"Yes, but it was about three weeks, and I hadn't stood up in a couple of days. Mom was horrified. She screamed and cried, but when she called the girl, she got only week excuses. They took me to Dr. R the next day. I could tell he was angry. He said my kidneys and liver were both shutting down so that he had no other thing to do but give me peace. Mom held me in her lap and cried. Dad petted me but said he couldn't watch. Doctor R. was so gentle and careful. I hardly felt the sting. I fell asleep my head on

Mom's lap as she stroked me. Her tears dampened my long, silky ears, and I woke up by the bridge."

"You poor dear. You didn't deserve such a fate. You earned respect and love." MoneyPenny felt so indignant. She assured Dottie she had a happy after life ahead, even if she didn't get into Heaven. She wanted to promise the setter she would seek justice for her, but worried whether she could find any solution and didn't want to bring any worry to the dog who needed to find solace and comfort in her new home.

Dottie the setter told the Ghost Horse her sad story.

CHAPTER 12

SENIORS FOR SENIORS

MoneyPenny snuggled into her red velvet bed on the side of Mom's bed. Her trip to the Rainbow Bridge drained all her energy and left her still looking for answers for her new friends' concerns. Mom stoked her with a warm, gentle hand. "I'm sorry you had such a stressful day with your new friends. Rest well, dear one. We have a big day tomorrow. It's "Clear the Shelters Day." The volunteers have cleaned and sprayed and even decorated all week. Sunday, we open at ten for people to come straight from early church to adopt a new pet. Vets have volunteered all week checking on vaccines and they sent their groomers and apprentices to brush and clean the animals. Pet stores have set up displays at the shelters and many even carried crates of small animals for displays welcoming customers to visit their stores."

MoneyPenny mewed a reluctant agreement. She buried herself in soft covers.

Morning came all too soon. Mom held her carrier open, and she darted in and turned to peer out the grating in the little door. Mom very kindly saved MoneyPenny's box to load last minute.

When they got out at the shelter, Ms. Alice had everything ready to open, MoneyPenny's job was to tour the place soothing any cats who seemed distressed at the unusual activity. "It's OK, Midnight, she purred to a nervous Oriental shorthair trying to fight her way out of her crate with its royal blue velvet curtain.

"What's going on?" she yowled softly, her voice shaky.

"Relax, You know Ms. Marcy will protect us. This is your chance to look beautiful and attract a new person to give you a forever home. You look so pretty with your fur wiped with sweet oil so you smell clean and look shiny."

The slim girl preened a moment under MoneyPenny's praise and encouragement.

The angel cat kept busy going by all the active cats to help them relax and settle in to wait for people to pet them. The place smelled of Pine-sol and lavender. Voices rattled with excitement as children ran to the kittens. Shrieks floated in from the distant hall where the dogs and puppies stayed. As the visits continued, the girls in the office kept typing and printing off the instruction forms and coupons for vet work that went in the adopters' welcome packets.

Ms. Marcy called, "MoneyPenny, here, girl." The tabby girl had barely caught her breath all morning. She bounded to Mom and rubbed against her leg. "Look up there at the second level, MoneyPenny," Mom said, pointing to the upper cages in the room of adult cats." She ran up the end cages to trot across the roofs of the top cages. The last four cages in the row had occupants. In each cage, a large cat reclined, clearly bored.

"Hey, guys and gals, you need to wake up and talk to your guests. People like cats who respond to them. The purpose of this party is to find forever homes for all our kitties. Don't you want a person of your own?"

As the older cats yawned and started explaining, MoneyPenny felt she had heard their stories before: "I had a wonderful home with a kind lady who loved me. Then one day, she didn't get out of bed. I even licked her Life Alert button until someone answered. But Mom couldn't talk to the person. I tried meowing. Apparently, the voice realized something was wrong. Emergency persons came and carried Mom away in an ambulance, but I knew she would never wake up. Her son brought me here."

As MoneyPenny projected the conversation, Mom got really sad. The Angel Cat felt her concern. Our problem cats, not because they are not sweet, but they are older and people want young, playful cats, or cats who don't have arthritis, or tummy troubles." MoneyPenny remembered an old lady coming in with her cane earlier. She tried to project to Mom what the lady looked like. She had told the girl at the door she wanted a cat that would sleep on her lap and not jump up on her table where her watercolors stayed spread out. A cat walking across a palette could make a real mess.

With help from Mom and her walkie/talkie to the staff, they found the old lady. She didn't take the beautiful Midnight, but she found the silver mackerel tabby fellow next to her appealing as he stretched and purred. He came with the name Moonsilver. His owner had been an old man writer who worked on a computer with a microphone to tell his stories. He rubbed against the lady and purred full volume. She fell in love.

Ms. Marcy got an idea from the senior kitties. As soon as the special day was over, the staff at the shelter had a lot to do sweeping out the empty cages to ready them for the next season's new residents. Marcy called the nearby assisted living facility. She offered to bring a cat to visit the residents. Some of them had their own cats or even dogs, but many had lost their pets and couldn't afford to adopt new ones. Marcy instructed their PR department to send a news release to the paper that senior citizens who wanted to adopt a senior cat or dog, over 8, could save the regular adoption fee.

"So, MoneyPenny are you ready for your new role? The old folks are so looking forward to seeing you." The tabby made sure her wings were secured deep into her fat pouch. She knew the old ladies' clutching fingers would not hurt, not really. Before they got into the common room at the facility, a lady with bright red hair reached toward MoneyPenny's carrier. "Is that a kitty cat? Can I pet your kitty? Please! I had a wonderful cat, but my family couldn't pay the pet fee here."

Ms. Marcy said, "This is MoneyPenny. She is here to visit today. We can let her out in your room."

The lady opened her door and waved them in.

As soon as the door closed, Mom set the carrier on a chair and opened its front. MoneyPenny knew better than to bound out. She stepped carefully to the front of the chair seat. The lady leaned to pick her up. To the cat's surprise, the lady lifted her expertly with a secure grip under her and held her against her cheek. She smelled of some kind of chewing gum and Jergens hand lotion. "Oh, you precious sweet girl, I wish you could stay. It's been a long time since I came here, and I never knew what happened to my Powder Puff. She was a chubby, Persian girl in buff and white fur…" She buried her face into MoneyPenny's stripes. The tabby projected a warm feeling to let the lady feel appreciated. "I could almost swear you have been talking to me.

After a while, Mom came to the door. "I'm sorry, but your neighbors have signed up for a turn with MoneyPenny. If there's time, we will stop back by on the way home. Thank you for your hospitality."

"Oh, I found a pack of Puff's favorite treats. Please let me give her some. Please!"

MoneyPenny thought she might like some if they weren't too stale, but Mom explained, "Our kitties are on special diets, so we don't let them accept food from anywhere else. Maybe you will get another cat sometime. Thanks." All day folks held MoneyPenny and petted her, and she heard more stories of pets sent to shelter when their owners had to go to a home. Some homes did allow pets, but most charged for the pet clean up, so some families claimed they couldn't afford the extra charge for their relative to keep her pet. MoneyPenny spied tears in Mom's eyes several times. When they got home, she read several articles on pets at nursing homes. She liked a series of books about a Maine Coon who was the resident at a rehab facility. He wandered from room to room offering himself for petting.

"MoneyPenny, do you think you could persuade one of our seniors to try being a nursing home cat?"

"Maybe. The lady cats probably wouldn't want to give up their independence. Let me visit them tomorrow."

As she trotted around the senior cat area at the Shelter the little tabby girl listened to the musings of the cats. Mr. Pepper, a domestic long hair fellow who had stayed in the shelter a long time seemed pretty discouraged. He thought an older couple planned to adopt him, but at the last minute one of the gorgeous white lady cats stepped in and managed to steal them away. MoneyPenny played to his sense of responsibility.

"Hey, Pepper, how'd you like a job?"

"What? We don't have jobs!"

"You could be chief welcome cat at the assisted living facility. They have people that get lonely and sad and need help with depression. Petting a cat, especially one that purrs, can lower their blood pressure. You would go visit various rooms to let people pet you. You might get picked up and put with someone particular, but mostly you go wherever you want."

"I've about given up on getting a home. Is this a home?"

"I bet you'd make friends, and they'll want you to stay," she told Mr. Pepper as she projected to Mom to get her help.

As she and Mr. Pepper went to the next room, a wizened old man leaned down, clearly in discomfort, to pet the long-haired tabby senior. "You look like you have been around the block a few times. How about resting here on this fancy pillow my granddaughter gave me when I turned eighty-eight." He lifted the hefty old cat with one hand underneath him and placed him on a brocade pillow in the high back antique rocker. He barely had room to sit beside the tired old cat.

Mr. Pepper felt a little overwhelmed. He couldn't count to eighty-eight, and he couldn't remember how much time had passed since anyone had lifted him just to pet him. His purr engine fired up without any planning.

MoneyPenny left him to go to the next room. She gleefully projected to Mom that the elder cat might have found a person to keep him. They would need to recruit another cat for the host cat at the nursing home. As she walked through the hall, past room after room, she noticed a strange aroma. Not everywhere. She tried to remember where she smelled it. Just there by the red-haired lady's door, she caught it again. She looked up at the many paintings the lady had on her walls. She loved painting flowers and pretty colors. One painting almost sparkled with light.

It had a rainbow, almost as prominent as the Rainbow Bridge. That was it! The Angel cat almost leapt into the air! She smelled that aroma when she was visiting the Rainbow Bridge. She didn't know how the smell could come to earth from that sort of obscure corner of Heaven. She determined to veer off by the little church to look for Dark Angel on her way home.

As she flew extra high toward the backyard of the church, she saw Dark Angel wrapping his trumpet and hymnal and New Testament into a corner of his robe to head for the Gates. "Wait! Please!" she projected as strongly as she could. Startled, he turned, peering toward the sky.

"Hey, Little Darlin'," he called. "Thought you were helping the nursing home learn the healing properties of cats."

MoneyPenny landed on the eave of the back porch. In a rush, she projected the complex result of her discovery. "How could a live person carry the aroma of the flowers by the Bridge?"

Her favorite angel bowed his head. Was he praying for the answer? "That sure is a strange problem. I've heard that some dogs, like the ones trained to scent out drugs or explosives, could tell when someone drew close to his final hours. Never heard of a cat doing it. That's all I can think of. I'll try to get Archangel Michael to explain it to me better. We angels learn some of the Holy Mysteries on a need to know basis. Meantime, you might visit with one of your police department's trained canine officers."

"Thank you so much, Dark Angel!"

She could hardly wait for Dad to go to his computer after dinner so she could think/talk with Mom about the whole day. Mom was fascinated with her news about the Red-haired lady's painting and the scent at her door.

"Dear little MoneyPenny, thank you so much for caring. You know Sergeant Adams, our neighbor, works in the Canine Corps, too. His dog Sport is a GSP, a black and white German Short-Haired Pointer. You've met him a time or two when you followed me on a walk. Remember he barked at you and sprinted to a sliding stop at the edge of the Adams yard."

She did remember the dog who was so amazed at her projection of images.

"Mom," she projected, "Could we go see him tomorrow? Please!"

So, they did, right after an early breakfast as Mike Adams took off on his run with Sport. Fortunately, Mom was also a runner, so as they joined the officer and his K-9, no one thought anything odd, "Hey, Mike, just the man I need to visit with," she called.

"Hi, Ms. Marcy, what's up?"

She said she had been at the nursing home and in preparing read some articles. Mike was not surprised at the articles on sniffer dogs detecting impending death. He said some homes even asked handlers to check on patients in hospice care. They could call next of kin, they could sometimes offer a patient a last wish. They could plan staff work schedules, mostly without upsetting anyone. Mom continued her run back toward the house. She took MoneyPenny back to the nursing home when she delivered the paper-work to finalize Mr. Pepper's adoption by the stiff old gentleman with the arthritis pain. It turned out the purring of the warm cat in his chair with him increased his relaxation and reduced his pain, thus lowering his blood pressure. Mr. Pepper had groomed himself better than any time in the last year. He meowed at Mom. MoneyPenny translated for her that he was saying thank you for getting him a new home.

She trotted off down the hall to find the red-haired lady. She hoped the strange floral fragrance would be smothered with Pine-sol today. She was so glad when she smelled the cleaning aroma, but just as Mom and the director lady caught up to her. Mom slowed to admire the many paintings in the hall and in the woman's room.

To their surprise Mrs. Betty met them at the door. "Is that the kitty I saw yesterday? I thought I was seeing things. I was so depressed. I missed my cat so much. He meant everything to me. She let me pet her. Could I really keep a cat here? I felt so much better. The little tabby girl gave me hope. She is such a positive little creature."

The little girl felt proud of helping the old lady. Could she have mistaken the smell when she saw the rainbow painting? The lady seemed a lot perkier than yesterday. Mom checked with the Director if Ms. Betty could afford the added pet fee. They determined she could, though her children do not see the necessity. As they turned to leave, they walked closer to the door across the hall while avoiding a laundry cart in the aisle. MoneyPenny smelled the floral scent again, stronger than yesterday. A lady lay in her hospital bed with the sides up and the head propped up. She whimpered. Mom shuddered. "That's the smell I got yesterday. It's stronger," projected the Angel cat.

"All I can smell is hospital and the irises in her vase and gardenias in the bowl."

"I wasn't wrong," MoneyPenny asserted. "She is the terminal patient. Do they already know that?"

About then, the old lady clearly moaned, "I want to go Home!"

The director suggested she was confused. She had lived there a year, so the nursing facility was her home now.

MoneyPenny hated to dispute the director's idea, but she projected to Mom, "She meant her Heavenly Home."

Ms. Marcy conferred with Ms. Betty about the fragrance and the rainbow and the painting and the neighbor's cry. Betty was so flattered that the cat thought of her painting with the Rainbow Bridge and assured mom that her neighbor was a very religious lady, so probably did mean her Heavenly Home.

A cat purring can ease high blood pressure.

CHAPTER 13

HELPING THE CAT IN THE WINDOW

MoneyPenny cruised the thermals and settled in an old crepe myrtle near a small frame house. She hesitated, unsure what had drawn her attention. Then she saw the cat in the window. She shifted to get a better look at the lanky fellow sitting just at the edge of the narrow venetian blinds. He wore his silver mackerel stripes with dignity, but his aura projected a lot of worry. MoneyPenny lighted close to the house and leapt to the brick ledge under the window.

"Hey, Silver Boy," she sent through the glass. "What's the matter?"

"I don't know where Mom has gone. Who are you?"

"I'm MoneyPenny. My mom volunteers at the animal shelter. She rescued me. Did your mom adopt you?"

"She took me in. That's a little different. I'd been visiting the clowder of cats who ate in her back yard off and on for a year. One cold night, I wondered if being inside might be better than shivering in one of the little cat houses she left out. When she went back to her door after setting down the food, I rubbed against her leg. She started talking to me and held the door. I trotted inside and she fell in love I think. Now she is gone. I can't get out to look for her."

MoneyPenny feared the poor fellow might be starving, but he anticipated.

"Her friends, one of the ladies from the vet clinic with Dr. Paul, a neighbor, Ms. Janice, and another lady take turns putting food out for us, me and White Kitty. She is a pretty little thing with a small black spot and calico tail. She is scared of the strangers, so runs under furniture whenever anyone comes in to feed us, or fill our water bowls, or clean our litter box."

"What happened?" MoneyPenny felt confused, glad at least he wasn't going hungry.

"About a week ago, Mom tripped and fell. She couldn't get up. White Kitty fled. Mom had a magic necklace she could talk to. Some strangers came in blue uniforms. They helped Mom onto a sort of bed they could carry. They took her out to a big white vehicle with flashing lights. I couldn't read the markings on it, but it sped away. I haven't seen Mom since. I don't know what has happened to her. I can't communicate with the people bringing us food. I guess the lady from the clinic knows me best, and sometimes she calls me Bentley. Her husband, our vet, gave me that name. I kind of like it, though Mom never uses it. I try to schmooze Dr. Paul when she comes, but she doesn't understand how worried I am."

"Gee, Bentley, that's tough. Don't know what I'd do if Mom disappeared," she said. She couldn't explain how she could communicate with people sometimes by projecting ideas to them and listening to their thoughts. Maybe she could get Mom to check with Dr. Paul for her. "I can't make any promises, but I can listen to the volunteers at the shelter. If I can find out anything, I'll fly right back here," she wished she hadn't said it that way.

Bentley gave a cat's version of a shrug. "I sure hope you can help me. I'm frantic to know what is going on with her."

MoneyPenny jumped into a shrub near the window ledge and ran to the end of the house. She tried to stay hidden until she could run along the roofline and lift off with her striped wings.

As soon as she landed on the balcony rail at home, she began thinking to Mom about Bentley and his fear for his mom.

"Hi, MoneyPenny. You sound stressed. What's happened?"

She looked into Mom's eyes and said a single "meow." That got her full attention, for the Angel Cat usually just projected thoughts for Mom to pick up.

She sent an image of Bentley as he paced in the window frame.

"Oh, poor fellow. Is he abandoned?"

"No. His mom fell and the EMT's came and took her somewhere for help. His vet apparently knows what happened because his wife who works in his clinic comes and brings food for Bentley and someone he calls White Kitty."

"Well, we can check with Dr. Russ to find the vet you're talking about."

MoneyPenny felt so happy that Mom was helping with Bentley's problem. She followed Mom to the table where her lady picked up her phone. She reviewed everything Bentley said. At last, she remembered the name, Dr. Paul. Mom picked it up and told Dr. Russ. Their vet did know the man. He volunteered to contact his colleague.

MoneyPenny swished her whiplike striped tail with excitement. Now, she needed to wait for him to call back.

But waiting is hard. She imagined all kinds of problems. Finally, a little after Mom and Dad finished supper and all the dogs and cats had eaten even earlier, the phone rang. Her ears focusing like radar, MoneyPenny leapt to the table where Mom left her phone.

"I talked to Paul. He says White Kitty is feral and his daughter is trying to catch her so she can let her meet Carissa's family of barn cats who are like a community cat clowder."

"But what about Bentley?" MoneyPenny wanted to scream.

Apparently, her thought's energy reached into the phone. Dr. Russ said, "The tabby cat is getting fed canned food left for both cats every other day and a generous supply of kibbles to last two or more days and someone cleans their litter box every three to four days. The lady is an artist named June Summers, and has been in hospital first from her fall, then a dry cough and sore throat which the hospital associated with mold. Dr. Paul and his wife have been taking care of her and getting whatever she needs. They think she needs to go into an assisted living facility. Several of her friends are working hard to find a nice place. Things are pretty complicated. Adult Protective Services opened a case. Dr. Paul thinks the plumber may have called them. So, this is as much as we know. He said she misses Bentley terribly but the rehab facility doesn't allow pets. A lot of assisted living campuses allow pets as long as the resident is able to care for the animal.

"Of course the lady just wants to go home. But he doesn't think she will be able to now the APS is involved. Fortunately, she does have a retirement program that he believes will support her through assisted living."

Mom started chatting with Dr. Russ, and MoneyPenny considered flying back to talk with Bentley. Before she could leave, Mom had closed the patio door. She thought about requesting an escape, but decided Mom had already helped her out a lot. Tomorrow would have to do.

MoneyPenny wondered to Mom what Dr. Russ meant when he spoke about Adult Protective Services. She had learned of Child Protective Services when they did a big "Clear the Shelters" last year. Some government office checked to make sure children were safe from abuse by parents or teachers. Some of the shelter volunteers helped keep track of kids in the Foster Care System. Some foster parents wanted to adopt a pet for the child to learn to care for an animal and take responsibility. The cat wondered how this agency is related to Adult Protective Services.

"Well, dear one, sometimes senior citizens need protection too. Maybe they have grown children who don't have time to take care of parents who are ill or forgetful. Some grown sons or daughters take money from their parents. Sometimes a business might cheat a senior citizen."

The cat thought the idea sounded hard. But a state agency could keep an old person from living in her own house if it needed too many repairs? She wanted Mom to look at Bentley's home. Maybe she could go to see Dr. Paul. She thought Mom could use that magic phone to find his clinic.

Next morning, MoneyPenny hurried to see Bentley. When she landed on the window ledge she sensed his body landing on the inside sill. She began thinking through the information she had from Mom's contact with Dr. Russ. Bentley's mom was not seriously injured though insecure on her feet. She was lonesome for him and upset away from her house. Of course, the little tabby could not tell her new friend where his mom actually was. He was kept in the house for his protection. Maybe if she could stay around until someone came, she could project an idea to his people to explain to him what was going on with his mom Ms. June.

Surprisingly, two cars pulled into the driveway. A small, red-headed lady hopped out of one. She carried a kitty carrier. MoneyPenny listened carefully trying to learn what the people had planned. She recognized images of tables and clothes and vet clinic scenes.

For the first time, she felt the presence of White Kitty. Her sympathy flowed to the dainty girl in her rich white fur. The young cat's heart raced in anxiety as the people entered the house. MoneyPenny hid in the vines that covered a section of the front wall. They smelled pungent. She felt her throat constrict. Her nasal passages clogged. She sneezed and her mucus flew as Knasher's did in the mornings. She heard the small cat scrambling inside the house. Bentley met the red-haired lady at the door.

"Talk to him about his mom," MoneyPenny projected as strong as she could.

"Janice, we need to find some clothes for June. And take some pictures of the cats. She really misses them." Said the smaller woman.

"These cats haven't eaten all the food we left," Janice commented.

"I don't think White Kitty likes poultry canned food." "You might not get any picture of her, either."

"Here, Bentley, let me take a picture of you to show your mama June."

MoneyPenny tried to read reactions, wondering if the striking silver fellow would pose. Sure enough, the ladies congratulated each other on attractive photos. As they carried boxes full of clothes and a makeup kit back to the cars, they commented they would take Ms. June to a new place.

Watching through the blinds, MoneyPenny saw Ms. Anne open the carrier on the piano bench and pick Bentley up. The Magic cat projected calming thoughts to her new friend. "It's OK, Maybe, they will take you to your lady. Isn't this lady from the clinic? If they need to keep you there it might be easier."

She sensed his tension. Ms. Anne stroked him and lifted him into the carrier. "Hey, Big Boy, we will take good care of you for your mom. She misses you terribly. We are finding her a safe place to live that will let you join her. You will be fine."

"Carissa wants to give White Kitty a home in her group of barn cats. They are healthy and happy with good food and safe places to snuggle down. They can welcome a new friend."

MoneyPenny had trouble figuring how much of the lady's comments Bentley could understand. While the ladies opened the car and adjusted the carrier and put the belt across it, she slunk under the car to interact with the big silver mackerel tabby. She projected confidence and the assurance they would keep him for his mom. She felt Miss Anne's comfort with the boy cat.

As the car doors closed, she sprinted into the shrubbery, already planning how to tell Mom the boy cat's story and enlist her aid.

She started to climb up a vine as Ms. Janice backed her car out of the drive. Then she remembered White Kitty. She pressed her face to the window glass trying to get a glimpse of the little girl. She tried to project her thoughts in straight cat-speak. The smaller cat clearly had little experience communicating with people. As she watched, a dainty white cat crawled from under a wing chair. Then she stood, causing her calico tail to flip loose with a few tan hairs floating around her.

"Hey, Pretty Girl, what are you so upset about?"

Startled, she asked, "Who are you? What's happening to Bentley? He protected me."

MoneyPenny answered, "He is going to your vet's. He wants to hear from your mom."

"I'm not sure she is my mom too. I know she has fed us a long time. She was awfully upset when my brother got hit by a car. He crawled all the way back to the garage to come home, but he was too badly hurt. Dr. Paul took his body away. It was awful. I feel so alone now."

"Bentley thinks his mom will want to keep you. Ms. Anne says her daughter has a group of community cats at her barn where you could be safe. Maybe you will find a new friend," MoneyPenny offered.

MoneyPenny pressed her face to the lower part of the window. The lady will be living in an apartment. It's down a hallway with a lot of doors. People who work there come in to mop and clean."

She sensed the soft white girl's confusion. She sent a mental image of someone mopping.

"That's a scary thing. Where would I hide?"

"Maybe in the bed or behind it?"

"I'd rather run outside. Maybe a barn wouldn't be so bad."

"They get meals every day. Ms. Anne thinks one of Carissa's could be your brother."

"I'd like to meet him," she sniffed and slid down to get under a big chair.

MoneyPenny couldn't help worrying about the young white cat with the wild memories.

That night, Mom contacted Miss Anne. She had trouble explaining how she came to know of Bentley. But Dr. Russ had already contacted her husband. Since she was known as the shelter lady, Ms. Marcy could express concern for any homeless cats or dogs. Soon, MoneyPenny heard a lively conversation going as the two ladies reminisced about pets they had loved over the years. And the subject of June Summers popped up. Anne and her friends had found an assisted living facility that would welcome June with Bentley. The lady would be so happy to see him again.

MoneyPenny purred in relief. She shot a quick thought to Mom about White Kitty. Ms. Anne laughed. "Our daughter Carissa has a whole community of cats at her barn. She even caught that crazy white kitty of June's." MoneyPenny leaned into the phone.

Paul is examining it and getting shots up to date so she can go into the community. Carissa thinks one of the boys Paul neutered for her last year is probably White Kitty's brother. Last year, June had several of her ferals fixed. Carissa adopted a couple and put them in her barn. Looks like White Kitty has a new home. Jean sort of realizes that timid kitten would not do well with people coming into her room at the facility."

MoneyPenny picked up the idea of people coming into a room with the wild-hearted girl cat. If she bolted out the door, she could get lost. With her fear, she might not be able to tell the ones trying to help her. Apparently, she wouldn't miss the lady as much as the lady would miss her.

As she strolled into the dining room, Mom made happy sounds of approval. MoneyPenny already sensed Mom's plans to recruit Dr. Paul to become an associate vet for the shelter. The little tabby felt warm inside, looking forward to getting to know Ms. Anne better. Maybe she could even help Ms. Janice to become attached to the cats in the clowder of cats in Ms. June's backyard. She could drop in with helpful thoughts a few days a week. She wondered if she could find the barn where Carissa kept her clowder of community cats. Would Dark Angel let any of the other Magic Cat Angels help a clowder of feral cats?

Bentley yowled from inside the window.

CHAPTER 14

SHELTER DOG FINDS A JOB

MoneyPenny and Mom sat on the couch, the cat munching a few treats from one of those treat packs she had ordered online. Mom sipped a light white wine from a graceful goblet. She felt they had earned a break after the work at the assisted living facility. MoneyPenny began her nightly grooming, working her tongue in between her claws to clean each paw. One stubborn sticky spot remained from her touring at the Clear the Shelters. Something she walked through in the dog section. It reminded her of that day when a couple of old dogs had no interest at the sassy cat floating through the hall in front of their kennels. She remembered what thought fled from her mind that day: Old dogs need a purpose too.

"Mom, Do you suppose pet lovers look at old dogs the same way they do old cats? Seems strange, but it could be."

Mom sat up a bit straighter. "You're right. We've known the problem for a few years. And when we took kitties to the nursing home, we met several happy residents with a small dog. What about those who couldn't afford the pet fee? I'm calling Ms. Adams first thing tomorrow."

"Great," the tabby thought back. "If I could find a time when the dogs are quiet, maybe I can slip in and listen to their concerns. I don't know about those big dogs, like retired K-9's. 'They scare me up close.'"

"They already have a lot of training. I wonder if one could become a therapy dog. Nobody can lean on a cat for balance. If Ms. Adams has a nurse or physical trainer who wants to work with a dog, we might have a new source of therapy."

"Do they have a backroom that could be converted?"

"To what?"

"A kennel room for a couple of therapy dogs. Unless a couple of residents would want to keep one at night. After all, the goal is to get them a home."

The Angel cat stretched and yawned.

"You're right, sweet girl. Time for bed. Dad's already asleep." She led the way to the bedroom and fluffed the red velvet cushion of MoneyPenny's bed at the foot of her kingsize mattress.

Next day when Ms. Marcy gathered her supplies to go for her volunteer shift at the shelter, she called to the cat on the bacony, "Want to come to work?"

MoneyPenny sprinted to Mom's car and leapt into the back seat. She had thought out a deal with Mom that she could choose between a kitty car seat or a cat carrier. The car seat let her see more of the scenery they drove through. Sometimes she studied how different birds flew, taking off and landing. The grackles fascinated her because their tails switched to a vertical plane when they flew, a rudder. She doubted her whiplike tail would have enough surface to be useful. She sniffed Mom's packages to try to find a preview of her plans for the day. Of course, she sniffed Mom's usual bag of treats.

When they arrived, Mom conferred with Ms. Alice about the dogs. Their friend confirmed the problem for the senior dogs. Mom had written a news story Seniors for Seniors. When she read it, Ms. Alice offered to take it to the local paper for their website. MoneyPenny wanted to start visiting dogs right away. Mom did get her thought wave and moved toward the dog area, calling to one of the girl volunteers. They sometimes called Lindy their "Doggie Candy striper." Mom used the excuse that they needed to see how the dogs controlled themselves since the girls had no idea of MoneyPenny's magic skills, her telepathic ability.

With Lindy leading her, MoneyPenny felt almost safe. She projected calming thoughts as they went to the adult dogs. First, they saw the small dogs, Yorkies and Dashunds and toy poodles. Even in this category, several senior dogs had lived in the shelter for a year or more. Take Sam, the grey and silver Yorkie with his Fumanchu mustache. Dispite his appealing features, prospective adoptors shied away after reading his age. MoneyPenny scoffed to herself, don't people know that the smaller the breed, the longer the life expectancy. "Hey, Sam, what if we call you Lord Sam or Sir Sam?"

"Don't think it will make a difference." The old fellow rubbed his nose on his front paw.

Then she asked, "Would you like to meet some old folks who like dogs and want to pet you?"

"If that's so, why haven't they come here?"

"They aren't well enough to get around. They all live in a place called Country Villas with nurses and helpers to take care of them, but they want to see you. Ms. Marcy can set it up."

"Would I be the only dog?"

"I don't know. Think you could convince one of your small kennel friends to come too?"

"Maybe. I can ask around."

All the conversation took place in front of Lindy. The dog had no idea he spoke with a cat. He kept looking at Lindy as a child might watch a vintrilloquist.

Soon Lindy's lunch break ended the exploration. Mom petted her tabby girl. She made note of Sam and his dashund friend. Both dogs over twelve.

"Mrs. Arnold at the Villas is interested to try our suggestion but doesn't have time until tomorrow. Let's see if Sergeant Adams has any K9 officer friends with a retiree K9 who needs a job. His shift just ended. When the officer heard Ms. Marcy's idea, he rearranged his schedule to meet her. She carried MoneyPenny to the car and settled her into her car seat. The police officer looked a bit askance at Marcy's companion.

"What's that for?" he asked.

"She is my patience tester. She won't scratch if they won't chomp."

The sergeant laughed. He led them behind his house to a kennel room with heater and a/c unit, running water for cleaning, large windows and wide doors so dogs can freely move from inside shelters to outside pens under a high roof. "I'm the only guy in this area with enough room for these retired guys. My kids take them walking everyday. Most are too arthritic to run, but they still look for commands to follow." His eyes showed his concern for his four boarders.

"Can they be adopted?" Mom asked.

"Generally not," he said. "After a lifetime chasing felons, it's hard for them to play with family members."

"What about a therapy job as a support dog in a harness with a handle?"

"I've never come across one, but they are very obedient. In some cases, they are mourning the loss of their human partner."

As all the people talk went on, MoneyPenny lay in a sprawl at the front post where two kennel runs ran side-by-side. She felt the K9 energy as one of the dogs noticed her. She felt in her fur his concern. "I'm an animal, too, no mind," she projected. The tan and black German shepherd next to them stalked toward them one step at a time. The Malinwaugh she first spoke to spun to face his neighbor.

The shepherd declared he did not want any part of some-one holding a handle on his harness.

"I don't know what that would be like. Sometimes Bossman's kid leaned on me, and it was kind of fun to see how strong I am holding him up. Maybe. Any way I could try it out and change my mind if I needed to?"

MoneyPenny assured him he could. She wasn't sure the dogs would want to hear about a cat's success. She projected the image of the lady in hospice and how the cat could tell she was close to her fate.

"I wonder if that's like drug sniffing. I used to do that at the airport. You mean a home like that could use such information?"

"They seemed excited when they heard the news. Seems people want to say good-bye to old friends or family. Nurses need to arrange schedules, so the place has enough help at such a time." She almost said something about the Rainbow Bridge and some pets remembering if their family stayed with them for the vet's final gift.

So, at the end of the day, Ms. Marcy and MoneyPenny had a schedule for a couple of small dogs to perhaps have a new person and one to become a greeter visiting residents who wanted to rock with a dog in their lap or take their walker on a tour through the garden with a doggie companion. They had a retired K9 a probable new job. Quite a lot to look forward to trying out at The Villas tomorrow.

MoneyPenny and Mom sat on the couch, the cat munching a few treats from one of those treat packs she had ordered online. Mom sipped a light white wine from a graceful goblet. She felt they had earned a break after the work at the assisted living facility. MoneyPenny began her nightly grooming, working her tongue inbetween her claws to clean each paw. One stubborn sticky spot remained from her touring at the Clear the Shelters. Something she walked through in the dog section. It reminded her of that day when a couple of old dogs had no interest at the sassy cat floating through the hall in front of their kennels. She remembered what thought fled from her mind that day: Old dogs need a purpose too.

"Mom, Do you suppose pet lovers look at old dogs the same way they do old cats? Seems strange, but it could be."

Mom sat up a bit straighter. "You're right. We've known the problem for a few years. And when we took kitties to the nursing home, we met several happy residents with a small dog. What about those who couldn't afford the pet fee? I'm calling Ms. Adams first thing tomorrow."

"Great," the tabby thought back. "If I could find a time when the dogs are quiet, maybe I can slip in and listen to their concerns. I don't know about those big dogs, like retired K-9's. "They scare me up close."

"They already have a lot of training. I wonder if one could become a therapy dog. Nobody can lean on a cat for balance. If Ms. Adams has a nurse or physical trainer who wants to work with a dog, we might have a new source of therapy."

"Do they have a backroom that could be converted?"

"To what?"

"A kennel room for a couple of therapy dogs. Unless a couple of residents would want to keep one at night. After all, the goal is to get them a home."

The Angel cat stretched and yawned.

"You're right, sweet girl. Time for bed. Dad's already asleep." She led the way to the bedroom and fluffed the red velvet cushion of MoneyPenny's bed at the foot of her king size mattress.

Next day when Ms. Marcy gathered her supplies to go for her volunteer shift at the shelter, she called to the cat on the bacony, "Want to come to work?"

MoneyPenny sprinted to Mom's car and leapt into the back seat. She had thought out a deal with Mom that she could choose between a kitty car seat or a cat carrier. The car seat let her see more of the scenery they drove through. Sometimes she studied how different birds flew, taking off and landing. The grackles fascinated her because their tails switched to a vertical plane when they flew, a rudder. She doubted her whiplike tail would have enough surface to be useful. She sniffed Mom's packages to try to find a preview of her plans for the day. Of course she sniffed Mom's usual bag of treats.

When they arrived, Mom. Conferred with Ms. Alice about the dogs. Their friend confirmed the problem for the senior dogs. Mom had written a news story Seniors for Seniors. When she read it, Ms. Alice offered to take it to the local paper for their website. MoneyPenny wanted to start visiting dogs right away. Mom did get her thought wave and moved toward the dog area, calling to one of the girl volunteers. They sometimes called Lindy their "Doggie Candy striper." Mom used the excuse that they needed to see how the dogs controlled themselves since the girls had no idea of MoneyPenny's magic skills, her telepathic ability.

With Lindy leading her, MoneyPenny felt almost safe. She projected calming thoughts as they went to the adult dogs. First, they saw the small dogs, Yorkies and Dashunds and toy poodles. Even in this category. Several senior dogs had lived in the shelter for a year or more. Take Sam, the grey and silver Yorkie with his Fumanchu mustache. Dispite his appealing features, prospective adoptors shied away after reading his age. MoneyPenny scoffed to herself, don't people know that the smaller the breed, the longer the life expectancy. "Hey, Sam, what if we call you Lord Sam or Sir Sam?"

"Don't think it will make a difference." The old fellow rubbed his nose on his front paw.

Then she asked, "Would you like to meet some old folks who like dogs and want to pet you?"

"If that's so, why haven't they come here?"

"They aren't well enough to get around. They all live in a place called Country Villas with nurses and helpers to take care of them, but they want to see you. Ms. Marcy can set it up."

"Would I be the only dog?"

"I don't know. Think you could convince one of your small kennel friends to come too?"

"Maybe. I can ask around."

All the conversation took place in front of Lindy. The dog had no idea he spoke with a cat. He kept looking at Lindy as a child might watch a vintrilloquist.

Soon Lindy's lunch break ended the exploration. Mom petted her tabby girl. She made note of Sam and his dashund friend. Both dogs over twelve.

"Mrs. Arnold at the Villas is interested to try our suggestion but doesn't have time until tomorrow. Let's see if Sergeant Adams has any K9 officer friends with a retiree K9 who needs a job. His shift just ended. When the officer heard Ms. Marcy's idea, he rearranged his schedule to meet her. She carried MoneyPenny to the car and settled her into her car seat. The police officer looked a bit askance at Marcy's companion."

"What's that for?" he asked.

"She is my patience tester. She won't scratch if they won't chomp."

The sergeant laughed. He led them behind his house to a kennel room with heater and a/c unit, running water for cleaning, large windows and wide doors so dogs can freely move from inside shelters to outside pens under a high roof. "I'm the only guy in this area with enough room for these retired guys. My kids take them walking every day. Most are too arthritic to run, but they still look for commands to follow." His eyes showed his concern for his four boarders.

"Can they be adopted?" Mom asked.

"Generally not," he said. "After a lifetime chasing felons, it's hard for them to play with family members."

"What about a therapy job as a support dog in a harness with a handle?"

"I've never come across one, but they are very obedient. In some cases they are mourning the loss of their human partner."

As all the people talk went on, MoneyPenny lay in a sprawl at the front post where two kennel runs ran side-by-side. She felt the K9 energy as one of the dogs noticed her. She felt in her fur his concern. "I'm an animal, too, no mind," she projected. The tan and black German shepherd next to them stalked toward them one step at a time. The Malinwaugh she first spoke to spun to face his neighbor. The shepherd declared he did not want any part of someone holding a handle on his harness.

"I don't know what that would be like. Sometimes Bossman's kid leaned on me, and it was kind of fun to see how strong I am holding him up. Maybe. Any way I could try it out and change my mind if I needed to?"

MoneyPenny assured him he could. She wasn't sure the dogs would want to hear about a cat's success. She projected the image of the lady in hospice and how the cat could tell she was close to her fate.

"I wonder if that's like drug sniffing. I used to do that at the airport. You mean a home like that could use such information?"

"They seemed excited when they heard the news. Seems people want to say good-bye to old friends or family. Nurses need to arrange schedules so the place has enough help at such a time." She almost said something about the

Rainbow Bridge and some pets remembering if their family stayed with them for the vet's final gift.

So, at the end of the day, Ms. Marcy and MoneyPenny had a schedule for a couple of small dogs to perhaps have a new person and one to become a greeter visiting residents who wanted to rock with a dog in their lap or take their walker on a tour through the garden with a doggie companion. They had a retired K9 a probable new job. Quite a lot to look forward to trying out at The Villas tomorrow.

I guess I could let seniors hold onto me.

CHAPTER 15

OLD HORSE RETIRING

MoneyPenny soared over the woods where she met the Barn cat named Bright Eyes in the stable of the riding academy. She still enjoyed her wings from the angels. As she drifted into the shade under some high limbs, the barn roof lay just below. Gee, she thought, I need to check in on Bright Eyes now that she is respected as the barn mouser. She landed on the peak of the roof and crawled through the loft window.

"MoneyPenny, so glad you're here!" cried the sturdy little grey shorthair as the tabby dropped to the aisle floor.

"Hi, Bright Eyes! Are you still getting treats when you catch a mouse?"

"I get treats from Susan whether I catch anything or not. Mr. Sam is not so generous, but he picks quality kibbles for me. Right now, I want you to meet my new friend. He's a horse. His name is Captain. He has a fancier show name, but the riding students call him Captain.

The two cats trotted off toward a shady paddock with a hay bag hanging on the fence. Beside it, a large bay horse stood munching. MoneyPenny felt at once an aura of concern around him. Some of the images fliting through his mind showed big jumps of striped bars, or a few outdoor scenes as he galloped through a pond, leapt uphill and jumped a big solid wall of railroad ties. Then new images came as a vet examined the horse. The man with the stethoscope around his neck lifted the powerful back leg and held it flexed tight, counting. "Twenty," MoneyPenny heard in the horse's memory. "Now trot him away. Quick!" She felt the soreness Captain remembered from his hips and back and his stifle joint too.

The big bay stretched his muzzle toward Bright Eyes. "Hey, Little Fluff. If I lie down again, would you walk along my back? You take my worries away."

"Sure. But MoneyPenny might be better at it. She is heavier than I am. Captain, this is my friend, MoneyPenny. She saved me by teaching me to catch mice. She runs around a lot and knows a lot of people stuff."

The big brown face with its soft skinned muzzle swiveled to touch MoneyPenny. "Hi, tabby lady. We had a tabby cat at one of the barns where I worked for a while. He was my friend. Made the rats shut up when I needed to sleep. I stomped my hoof at the dog when she started to harass him."

"Nice to meet you, Captain. You are very impressive."

"Good, that's part of my job to impress judges. Hope I'm still up to it." With that, he shook himself, throwing a cloud of dust into the air. He turned around on the grass, pawed once, and folded his front legs to slide to the ground.

"C'mon, MoneyPenny," Bright Eyes mewed and hopped to the big brown hip. Captain swished his thick black tail, almost catching MoneyPenny as she arrived beside Bright Eyes. The little grey girl motioned with her chin, and the tabby followed her lead. They walked side-by-side along the horse's spine, sheathing claws and pressing paws into the soft brown hair along his back muscles. MoneyPenny felt the big creature's muscles relaxing. If he were a cat, he'd purr. The two cats felt good making him feel better.

But she still sensed his overbearing worry tinged with fear. What was he so worried about? She used cat perception to communicate with Bright Eyes outside the horse's awareness. The little barn cat contributed how he came back from his show last week with his back leg wrapped and had to stand for the vet to stretch his limbs. The stable workers hosed down his legs every day. The cats decided to ask him outright what had him so upset. As they marched their way from his withers back to his hip, they purred to Captain to reassure him.

They hopped to the ground behind the big horse. He stretched his front legs forward and scrambled to his feet. He turned around to thank them. "Oh Captain, we can't do what the chiropractor can. Do you think your owner will go for that treatment?"

"My owner is a trainer. He had me teach his students and carry them through events. He will pay for treatments that make me able to perform better. This injury is different. I've had minor strains and bruises over the years, but this one I'm not coming out of to go back to work. Maybe I could tote a small child, but I couldn't jump anything more than a foot or so and couldn't do any lateral work for dressage. I'm old enough that I can't be sold for the price I would have brought last year. Trainers can't afford to retire their old workhorses. I just hope I don't get sold to one of those buyers who shove too many horses into a truck to Mexico." He shuddered. The cats looked at each other. They knew some pet shelters killed excess animals when they got crowded. Ms. Marcy never did that at her shelter. Did Captain think his owner was going to take him to a killer auction?

"What can we do?" They asked.

"Nothing. I can't run away. I guess I can just eat my feed and hope. Maybe one of you could write an ad for me like on one of those dating sites. 'Beat up old horse offering to work as lawn mower. Possible wood working. Modeling for photos and artwork.'"

The cats realized to their horror, he wasn't kidding. This powerful figure stood with his noble head hanging listless. He slouched, resting his left rear leg.

"Does your leg hurt a lot?" she projected.

"It's a little better. My boss isn't asking me to work anymore. Maybe rest will help. The hydrotherapy helps."

"School's out," Bright Eyes announced. MoneyPenny looked up. Two cars pulled into the parking lot; doors flew open and three youngsters bounded out squealing with excitement. Their boots clumped on the concrete aisle.

"Where's Captain?" someone yelled.

"Look, he's in the paddock!" All three kids ran toward the horse and his cat friends. "I've got peppermints!"

"I've got horse treats, apples and carrots!"

MoneyPenny thought she could leave the horse to go tell his story to Mom. "See you tomorrow, Bright Eyes."

On hearing the story, Ms. Marcy went online looking for horse charities. The race horses had a retirement foundation. Harness horses had one. Arabians had one. Many states had rescue groups for horses. Donkeys had one. Even Mules had one. The US Equestrian Foundation and Dressage Foundation gave grants to prospective young riders and their prospective horses. But for sad old lesson horses who came on hard times, no one seemed to realize the extent of the problem.

"Those kids sure had fun feeding him treats. Maybe someone could open a horse theme roadside zoo. 'Free petting. Bring your own treats,'" the Magic Cat suggested. Dad and Mom discussed the problem over dinner.

Dad swept his fork across his pie plate to save the last crumb and wedge it into the cheddar cheese. He did like apple pie. He leaned back in his chair. "I can still drive a trailer. What about persuading the owner to let us take him to a show and see if some of the parents or mature riders will help us fund his retirement. We could have an 'Adopt a show horse,' campaign. Maybe set up a go-fund-me page for him"

"What a great idea. We already have the 501c for the shelter. We could rescue horses. We just wouldn't have room for more than two."

"You need to get an artist involved to make you a banner we can hang on our trailer at a show and maybe on front gate when we're home."

"This is great for Captain and a single companion, but we cannot save all the horses who need saving. We have to recognize reality."

As they thought about Captain, the local news featured a county horse show. In a blatant attempt for public appeal, the reporter focused on the lead line class. Riders had to be under ten. The leaders had to be at least 15 and hold a line to the horse at all times, but the child must hold reins all the time and riders must have feet in stirrups. Bonus points for posture and smile. Proper clothes either English or Western could also add appeal. Some creative moms select matching outfits.

"Isn't that darling! Mom cried, pointing. She had not had children, but helped bring up Dad's son. The boy was almost retirement age by now. Dad watched a couple of minutes.

"Need a nice horse for that. Sometimes a little kid riding a big horse well get favorable attention," he contributed.

MoneyPenny was so excited. She dashed to the balcony and disappeared into the night. As she landed at the stable, she called to Bright Eyes, "Quick, where is Captain. I think I can get him a new job."

Bright Eyes dropped the mouse she just dispatched. "He's turned out. Now that he doesn't bring in revenue, the boss doesn't want to spend money paying to have his stall cleaned. He does get good meals, though," she added to be fair. The two cats tumbled across the lawn to the paddock. Thy could just make out Captain's large form on the ground in the warm sand.

"Captain, how do you like little kids?" MoneyPenny demanded.

"Huh? I was sleeping. Mr. Sam gave me a little Bute, and I quit hurting so I could sleep."

"We won't take long, old friend," Bright Eyes said. "You can go back to sleep. Listen to what MoneyPenny heard on TV."

The tabby explained how cute the kids were and how small, so not very heavy. "And all they do is walk!

The announcer said good lead line horses sell for good money! I bet Mom can find someone to take you to a show as a lead line horse." The sleepy horse struggled to his feet and shook himself while he tried to absorb the prospect of a new job.

"It might work," he said slowly. "I almost resigned to being abandoned in a back field or getting prodded into the cattle truck. I'm afraid to hope. Thanks, cats. At least kids bring treats."

MoneyPenny rubbed along his leg and purred. She remembered she still had to convince Mom. "See you soon, Captain." She darted back into the barn headed for the loft.

As she flew home, MoneyPenny considered consulting Dark Angel. She hoped Mom would take her online to look at some rescue horses. She wondered how Bright Eyes could get Ms. Susan to find out what kind of money the trainer thought he had to get for his big bay gelding. Maybe they could find some horse magazines to look at ads for lead line horses. She might have to get Mom to read the small print ads to her. She knew she wasn't a good reader.

Step one was to get Mom to help look for ads. She knew she was too late to do it tonight. She tried to think who had a child under ten who might want to take a lead line horse to a show. She thought about praying for help. Somewhere she heard, "Ask and ye shall receive." Was that in the Bible? She wasn't sure what the big black book was for. When she slipped into the house, she hopped on Mom's bed and purred. She projected her concerns to Mom as the dawn lit the window sill.

"Mom," she called with her heart. She felt they had to learn where shows had these lead line classes and needed to find some ladies with young kids they want to show off. Mom didn't show horses, didn't even ride much. Could she pretend to be a prospective customer for Captain's owner? Bright Eyes learned from the barn dog the man's name, Dave Reynolds. She thought Sam had been the stable boss because he made decisions about the rats and the barn cat. He is the live in groom, her friend learned.

Mom promised to stop by the feed store where the shelter did business. She could ask the people there about these special classes. Also, they had ads on their bulletin board for some equine rescue sanctuaries. "Can I go with you?" MoneyPenny begged. She never asked that before, but Mom had taken her to check the police dogs being retrained. The little tabby put on her sweetest face. Ms. Marcy put her hands on her hips.

"How can any animal lover resist such an appeal?"

When Mom got ready to leave, she held the car door for her cat to bound in. She crouched in the passenger foot well. Soon, she gave in to the temptation to look out windows. She crawled and climbed to the back seat to hold on right by the window. As they rolled into the open parking lot, amazing smells assailed her. Everything from rat bait to fly spray to chicken droppings! A black bantam rooster crowed with arrogance! He stood in a crate over a screen frame. Nearby three red hens pecked at a feeder in another crate. Bubbles gurgled in a tub of water teaming with minnows and a few goldfish. Signs tried to lure people to check lighted incubators with baby birds—chicks, ducklings, even a couple of tiny turkeys, all chirping or quacking or hissing.

"You have to stay here," Mom ordered. 'They have dogs that would go crazy to see you. I'll get copies of magazines and take pictures of ads that look interesting," she promised. When she went inside the store, MoneyPenny stood in the window and focused on her mom.

Ms. Marcy picked up a new issue of the *Rider's News*. One feature article showed "What's new in Leadline?" She tucked it under her arm. Another magazine offered, "How to evaluate a horse rescue?" That got shoved inside the first publication. Of course, Mom had to chat with various folks she recognized. Never hurts to spread the news. People knew Captain from his shows. One neighbor showed some enthusiasm about leadline for a grandchild. She just went to a show with the child all dressed. She carried a pair of children's stirrups with a split strap to fit over the pommel of the Western saddle. Surprising how many people would lend her a horse to put in the class.

Mom returned to the car with the two publications and a box of vaccines for the shelter animals. They planned to study with Dad that night. The Angel Cat flew to the stable to get the latest news from Captain and Bright Eyes. The horse stood in the shade by his nearly empty hay net. She detected no gleam of hope. "My boss led me out today. He just shook his head. I don't think the people expect me to get well."

"Maybe you can surprise them. If Mr. Sam gives you more Bute, you might be able to go sound. There are exercises people use to get flexibility back. I bet there are some for horses. Maybe Mom can find some online."

The tabby thought of Mom's voice reading stuff she found online. "Thoroughbreds had a rescue association." She knew those were horses who ran in races for people to bet on. If one just ran too slow or got too upset at the big metal starting gate or ran into other horses or let his jockey fall off too much, trainers had trouble keeping him at the track. Not many owners would take a horse like that home to become a riding horse. However, some did get sold to hunter/jumper trainers. They called them OTTB's: Off-Track ThoroughBreds. What if Captain were one of those? He would have a whole organization wanting to rescue him. Would his trainer care or want to get help for him?

Seemingly out of nowhere, MoneyPenny asked, "Captain, were you ever a race horse?" That might not be a good point to list for a Leadline horse, but if it opened a source of help, it would be worth knowing.

"I don't know. Seems like I remember getting to run my fastest sometime when I was very young, barely saddle broke. Someone on a big sturdy horse led me onto soft dirt. Sometimes, I didn't even have a rider. Then a young kid started riding me with a tiny saddle strapped on with a sur-cingle. Then something happened and my front legs really hurt. They rubbed numbing cream on them and poked hot needles clear to the bone. I don't remember very well because I was doped up with something they called 'Ace.'"

"Sounds like you were started toward racing but broke down. Mom's research called that 'pin-firing.' Thank goodness, they have better treatments now. The hydrotherapy, just squirting cool water on your legs would heal them. Isn't that what they are doing for you now?"

"Yes. It depends who holds the hose how long and how thorough it is. Why did you ask about all this?"

"If we can prove you are a Thoroughbred, the Thoroughbred Rescue Sanctuary may step in and help you have a place to retire. Maybe I could check your legs and find the needle marks."

"Hmm. I guess you can see, if you want. I'll try to stand still. Tell me when you change legs. If I get tickled unexpectedly, I might jerk the leg. Don't want you stepped on."

As the sun began to set, the Angel Cat rubbed her chin up the horse's front leg. She wondered sometimes how these slim legs could land in jumping or galloping with the whole weight of the horse on a three-inch diameter foot. She started at the hoof and licked the fur the wrong way, trying to test the smoothness of the skin, seeking the now miniscule thickened specs of scars from the needle punctures years ago.

"I can't be sure. At your age and with all your cross country work, you figure to have some marks. Maybe a vet could tell. If I could be in the barn when the vet checks your progress, maybe I could suggest he be curious about old injuries or treatments."

"Dr. Cathy is our vet's new helper. I think she's smart, and she likes me. I feel her kindness and her hopes for me. I don't see how you could affect what she does."

Bright Eyes interrupted, "When Sam wanted to starve me into catching mice, she convinced Susan to speak for me. She gave her ideas how cats need nutrition to hunt. I don't know how she does it, but she has some kind of magic."

"OK, but how can we tell her when they're coming?" the tired old fellow asked.

"Let me work on that. Maybe Mom can get Dr. Russ to help her with research. He might be able to make use of a veterinary intern in the area."

MoneyPenny. Counted on the planned conference with Dad tonight. If he and Mom get online, she felt confident she could think suggestions to Mom, maybe fill her in on the treatments and the possibility Captain could be a Thoroughbred.

That night brought up as many questions as answers. Mom put one of the laptops on the internet to the Thoroughbred Rescue Sanctuary and left it open for MoneyPenny to play with. She had to learn to place one of the pads on her front paw on the word. No claws, no fur, just a warm dry pad. She looked at "Who We Are" to learn which horses they would rescue. Easy if the horse was leaving from a track. But most Thoroughbreds who went into riding careers carried their papers with them, so owners had records. She also hit, "What can we do for the retiring horse?" She saw pictures of horses at farms in states from California to New York to Florida, as well as Kentucky. Of course, they all looked happy grazing in green fields with safe fences. She thought Captain would like that. Was Mom's field and small loafing shed enough pasture? A short video showed volunteers retraining a racehorse to go quietly for an amateur rider. She didn't think Captain needed that.

Finally, she tapped, "Horses for Adoption." Over a hundred horses had photos and descriptions along with price tags. Despite her confusion on reading, she found they were in farms in a lot of states. She didn't think Captain could be adopted if he couldn't carry a rider. They had a category, "Companion." Since horses are herd animals, they do not do well alone. Sometimes, someone needed a second horse to keep their show horse happy.

Dad decided to confer with Dr. Russ. MoneyPenny knew her vet to be a very nice man and thorough research person. She listened carefully when they talked.

Dr. Russ already knew the intern from her directing vet, Dr Sloan, bringing her to the county veterinary association meeting. He offered to suggest a brief research project for her featuring Dr. Sloan's patient Captain. He and Dr. Sloan had been friends for years, so he thought he could work with her for a visit. He had once been a track vet himself, so had contacts with Thoroughbred Rescue. With Mr. Reynolds' cooperation, he felt sure he could get help for Captain.

MoneyPenny will know when Dr. Russ goes to look at Captain because he will call Mom at the shelter. She loved telling the big bay horse how many people were helping. If he had to retire from lessons, he had a place to go. Not a truck to Mexico. He admitted he did not think his owner would really send him to a kill auction.

Finally, the call came. Mom drove home from the shelter to pick up MonyPenny, letting her sit on the back seat. At the farm up the road, the Angel Cat bounded out and headed for a stall in the barn where she could see Captain standing in crossties in the aisle. Dr. Sloan was new to the cat. His assistant was also new, the first lady the cat saw as a vet. She hoped the young woman liked cats. Bright Eyes heard her idea and assured her, "She keeps a pocket full of cat treats."

The two cats strolled into the aisle, tails floating behind. Captain flicked his ears at them. MoneyPenny heard Dr. Russ drive to the barn entrance. She looked up at her tall vet. He introduced himself to Dr. Cathy with a casual wave to Dr. Sloan. He asked Cathy, "Suppose your client wanted to confirm his horse is a Thoroughbred, what can you do?"

"Look at paper work simplest way. If the horse is supposed to have been on the track, we could check for tattoo under lip. If we think the horse may have left the track after a bowed tendon, we could look for pinfiring scars, depending on time, of course. And we can pull mane hairs and send follicles to A&M with $65 to get a DNA test. It will tell four or five most prominent breeds behind the horse. Are you concerned about this horse?" She felt confident she covered all the bases. Dr. Sloan looked pleased too.

"Good job," Dr. Russ admitted. "Want to look for those marks?"

She looked at her director. Dr. Sloan smiled and nodded. "They might be too old to find, so you are not being tested, Cathy."

She shrugged. "OK, Glad to try." She stepped to Captain's shoulder and spoke to him. He aimed his left ear at her. "OK, Big Horse, I need to check your leg." She knelt beside his foreleg. Her hand wrapped over the front of the cannon bone. She slid it slowly down the leg to the fetlock. She worked it back up, rubbing under the hair, turning up the clean white hairs. "Captain is eighteen years old, so if he left the track as a two-year-old, the scars would be sixteen years old. With all the nutrition and grooming over the years, I doubt I can find any marks."

Captain snorted. MoneyPenny picked up his feelings as he realized the girl had done something special for him. He nibbled at her hand as she fed him a treat.

Dr. Sloan asked Dr. Russ, "Is it OK to cheat and look at the registration papers? Mr. Reynolds keeps a copy in my computer files. Why did you need to know?"

"Some of the kids are afraid if he can't get well, he might be sent to the auction where killer buyers hang out. One of the mothers found Thoroughbred Rescue, but didn't know if Captain is a Thoroughbred. Sorry, I've never met your client, so didn't feel I had a right to demand what his plans are for the horse."

About then, the door up the hall opened and a man in tall boots strode toward them. "Hi, Doc, what's with all the crowd? Has his injury developed a weird complication I missed?"

"No, Dave, just a research opportunity for my intern and a chance to share a visit with a colleague. Dave Reynolds, meet Dr. Russ Macky. You might want him in your emergency list in case I'm on another call or playing with grandchildren." The tall man and Dr. Russ shook hands expressing cordial respect.

"Well, how's Captain coming along?"

"We're just about to trot him out. Dr. Cathy would you like to lead him for us, or do you prefer to observe?"

"I'll be glad to lead him. He's a neat horse. I think I can feel his energy level as a big clue to how he feels, but maybe Mr. Sam can do a quick line for me to watch before we turn him loose,"

"Sure, Young Lady," the silver-haired groom agreed. The cats hid in a stall to watch through the boards.

The student vet unclipped the cross ties from Captain's halter. The metal snaps clunked against the stall walls when she dropped them. His ears flicked as she untied his lead rope from around his neck. She walked purposefully to the end of the concrete aisle and turned back. "Trot, Captain, come on." She gave a gentle tug. The horse glanced at her. She tugged again and began trotting herself. He lifted himself into a sedate version of a trot. With her left hand, she flicked the tail of her lead rope toward the big bay hips. Captain coughed a soft nicker and picked up his pace slightly. His left rear leg clearly dragged a shorter strep than the right one.

Dr. Russ exchanged a clear look with Dr. Sloan. "Dr. Cathy, think that's far enough for right now. We've seen all we need for evaluating. In his defense, standing for a while may have let him stiffen up. Rest him a few minutes. Then maybe Mr. Sam can walk him up and down. Sometimes a little walk can loosen him up. If you like, I will pro bono show you and the horse's groom some stretches that may help over the long term."

Clearly, the girl wanted to accept his offer. She looked to check with Dr. Sloan and with the senior groom. They both moved toward Captain. She handed the lead to Sam who reached his gnarled hand. The cats slipped down the aisle closer to the big bay.

The gelding looked confused. Were the vets going to prescribe any pain management meds? Was this new vet a chiropractor? Could he really help? He rested his chin on Dr. Cathy's shoulder. Her hands petted his neck below his ears and worked down the cheeks to the muzzle. Dr. Russ smiled as he took the horse's lead.

"Ironically, even though we know specifically where the injury is, the first thing to do is unlock the neck." He demonstrated pulling his head around to the left. Dr. Russ pushed his elbow mid-neck into the rich brown hide. As his other hand pulled the jaw around, keeping it down, everyone heard a crack like a pistol shot. Captain gave a small startle reaction then as Russ dropped the lead, he stretched his neck downward. Then he repeated the action to the right. "Let me use some of your treats," he asked the girl. She dug a handful from her pocket, Captain's ears showed immediate interest. He lured the horse to stretch straight up, then down. He took a position beside Captain and lured his nimble muzzle to his elbow then to his hip, stifle, and hock. Then he coaxed the horse to get a treat from between his front legs. "Now, Dr. Cathy, you do the other side. If people would do this routine before and after every ride, they'd be amazed how flexible their horse will become."

"Now, Mr. Reynolds, before I perform any chiropratics with your horse, I need your consent to treatment."

Dave stretched his arms over his head. "I use a chiropractor myself. I don't know if I can afford one for my horses. I appreciate the offer. I'll have to consider any long term project. Thank you very much."

Dr. Russ stepped to the rear leg. He lifted it and flexed the hock until Captain objected with a polite tug. "That's enough for now. Now Mr. Sam, try it." The senior groom stepped to Captain's rear leg. As he lifted it. Dr. Russ corrected his grip. "It gets easier if you can get your hip under it. You want to listen to your own muscles. If you get tired, the horse will be tired too. Do this before you hose him down and after, before you turn him out. He needs pasture rest. He will stock up if you keep him in stall more than a couple of hours."

With that, Dr. Russ waved farewell walking to the door. Dr. Sloan and his intern packed up too, leaving Dave and Sam and Susan, who had slipped in about halfway through. She looked at Dave. "Would you ever sell a horse at one of those auctions?" she whispered.

Dave took the lead from Sam and moved to his horse's head. He put a treat in his palm and held it for Captain. The big brown head with its small, centered star dived into his master's hand. He crunched, almost smiling. Dave petted the strong neck and whispered into the ear swiveled toward him, "I'll never send you somewhere bad, Ole Man."

MoneyPenny felt her horse friend would be all right, even if his leg did not heal enough for him to continue his show career. She had learned as Bright Eyes showed her the whole farm, that a few horses lived in a back field with water and piles of hay. They didn't get grain or fancy supplements but the grass was high and they had shade trees and water troughs that filled automatically every morning. The barn cat recalled a time or so when snow became fierce, workers brought the horses into the covered arena for shelter and even put blankets on them to turn them out for the day. As she trotted past Captain on her way to fly home, he nickered to her, "Thanks, MoneyPenny."

Captain's trainer saved the day.

EPILOGUE

HAIKUS FOR MONEYPENNY

Stripes soft as contrails
Float across sunset fur
Gold gliding motion.

Her spots like shadow
Patterns splattered across
Leafy forest trail.

When cold, she
Huddles in muff position
A soft warm cushion.

Sometimes she meows
Her merry clear demands
Purrs subliminal.

Moneypenny believes most cats share magic.